Maria Simpson

Brother G.M. Rose

A temperance story

Maria Simpson

Brother G.M. Rose
A temperance story

ISBN/EAN: 9783337141493

Printed in Europe, USA, Canada, Australia, Japan

Cover: Foto ©Andreas Hilbeck / pixelio.de

More available books at **www.hansebooks.com**

"BROTHER G. M. ROSE;"

A Temperance Story.

BY

MARIA SIMPSON.

Toronto:

HUNTER, ROSE & CO., PRINTERS, 25 WELLINGTON ST,

1879.

To the Master,

WHOM OUR BROTHER, G. M. ROSE,

LOVES AND SERVES SO WELL,

This Little Book

IS EARNESTLY DEDICATED BY

The Author.

PREFACE.

THE author has greater need than ever to entreat the forgiveness of Mr. G. M. Rose, not only for making use of his public utterances in favour of Total Abstinence and Prohibition, but also for transferring to paper some slight glimpses of himself. The principal reason for this may be found in the ritual of the Sons of Temperance. It was in order that others might follow his example and learn to imitate his virtues.

CONTENTS.

—o—

"BROTHER G. M. ROSE."

CHAPTER I.

PHRENOLOGY.

"HEAR of it again in Heaven, will he!" exclaimed Miss Wood in a peevish tone; "well, may be so, I don't know."

Mrs. Somerville looked surprised. "The Bible says that even a cup of cold water will be remembered;" she earnestly answered, "and therefore, it is impossible that the noble Prohibition speech of Mr. Rose, to the reform clubs from up north, will be suffered by our Lord Jesus to lose its reward."

"I'll not dispute it," grimly replied the spin-

B

ster; "now be good enough to give me a synopsis
of the other addresses, and not any more of *his*."

Her niece complied with alacrity, and gave a
tolerably fair account of the remarks of Rev. Dr.
Cassel and Mr. T. H. McConkey.

"Hattie," said Miss Wood in surprise, "how
could you pay such close attention to outside matters, on the very day that you had gotten your
engagement ring?"   ·

Mrs. Somerville reddened.   With a half-laugh,
she replied, "Do you suppose that a dozen engagement rings would make me forget the Temperance cause?   No, no, Aunt Fanny, never you
think it!"

Some days afterwards, when the Club met as
usual in the Albert Hall, a phrenologist was present, who, instead of making a speech, agreed to
examine the head of the Temperance lecturer, Mr.
T. H. McConkey.   He did so, and gave the details
to the audience.   Then as he had met Mr. Mc-
Conkey before, he offered to read the head of some
gentleman with whom he was entirely unacquain-
ted.   The chairman at once asked Brother Rose
to allow his head to be examined, and the audience

clapped their hands. Mr. Rose good-naturedly consented, though he had never undergone the ordeal before.

" How very unpleasant it must be," whispered Hattie to her aunt. " Mr. McConkey went through it with great coolness and evidently did not mind it in the least." ·

Mr. Rose came forward, ascended the platform and seated himself in the arm-chair. His face was painfully flushed before the phrenologist even touched him, and continued so all the time. But he retained his usual playfulness and remarked, " This gentleman is not acquainted with me, and fortunately does not know what a hard case I've been."

" That is just like Mr. Rose," whispered Hattie, with a laugh. " While so many here are reformed men, he has been Temperance from his childhood ! I wonder if that man will ever find it out."

The phrenologist commenced by telling Mr. Rose that the " love of approbation " was strong in him. He had a good share of ideality—was always ready to speak—would come right to the

point and " was not in the habit of polishing off his
sentences." Mr. Rose smiled at the latter remark
—it was certainly true. The phrenologist spoke
highly of his mental powers—said that he would
not be afraid or shrink in the moment of danger,
but in business matters he was a cautious man,
and would first ascertain that all was right and
satisfactory in plans and projects, after which he
would " go ahead." The organ of veneration was
not so well developed as the others. He would
not bow the head to anyone—did not think anyone
his superior—he would not give way or bend his
will to another. However, he had quite enough of
veneration to make him a good Christian and
church-member. " You do not drink," continued
the phrenologist, " and have not been a dissipated
man—you are too fond of making money for
that." Mr. Rose smiled. " The organ of benevol-
ence was largely developed in him, and he was
very liberal in cases of distress. It was easy to
touch his heart in that way. Friendship was
also well developed ; but in argument, or when
anyone vexed him, he could speak sharply.
He would not use abusive language, was not

aggressive, but would say things in a style that meant business"!

When the phrenologist had finished his examination, Mr. Rose gave him a hearty "Thank you," and came down from the platform. Towards the close of the proceedings, he was called upon to make the appeal, which he did in his usual earnest manner.

"I wonder" said Miss Wood, on her return home, " whether Mr. Rose, felt as uncomfortable as he looked. Why, Mr. McConkey did not change colour in the least, but Mr. Rose's face was flushed to the roots of his hair."

"It must have been unpleasant," answered Hattie. "He was very good natured to comply with the wishes of the audience."

"The remarks were favourable enough," continued the spinster, peevishly, " so, why need he have been so confused ? As for intellect, it needed no phrenologist to tell us that he has plenty of it. What are you laughing at, Hattie ? Do you suppose that because I like neither Mr. Rose, nor his Prohibition addresses, I cannot speak the truth ? It is very probable that a finer intellect

than his does not exist; a single glance at his
high, broad forehead, will tell you so, without a
phrenologist going to the trouble of examining his
head! Now just stop laughing—how silly you are!
Do you imagine for a moment that his mental en-
dowments are any credit to Mr. Rose? Not they,
indeed. Who gave him that splendid intellect I
would like to know?"

"God," promptly replied Hattie; "and Mr.
Rose has not let the gift run to waste. He has
cultivated it and used it for God and humanity."

"The phrenologist was not correct in everything," remarked Ronald.

"No," answered Hattie, "I thought my ears
must have misled me when he said that Mr. Rose
could not speak fluently. Oh, did I not wish that
the man was supplied with pencil and paper and
bidden to take down one of those glowing addresses? What nimble fingers he would need to
keep pace with Mr. Rose! Why, one can hardly
do it in thought, for he is so eloquent, and thinks
and speaks quickly."

"The phrenologist was quite mistaken," remarked Ronald; "and also I believe in his state-

ment about the 'love of approbation.' Once I chanced to be present when an earnest 'Son of Temperance' pronounced a glowing eulogy on Mr. Rose, who sat with his head resting on his hand, as he does when thinking deeply, and I really don't believe he heard the half of it!"

"What is there wrong in the love of approbation?" grimly inquired the spinster. "It is only the reckless and bad who care for neither God nor man."

"That is an altogether different phase of the subject," replied Hattie. "I do not know whether the phrenologist was correct or not; but this is certain, all the praise or blame in the world would not make Mr. Rose swerve a hair's-breadth from the path of duty."

Two weeks passed.

"Mr. and Mrs. Tom Harding are going to attend our Club, to-night, aunt," remarked Mrs. Somerville; "they belong to the one in the West End, you know."

"Then you can surely dispense with me."

"No! indeed; we want all we can get."

Miss Wood, with a sigh of resignation, accordingly accompanied her niece.

Just before the meeting commenced, Mr. Rose entered the hall.

"You're a deceiving thing, Hattie," angrily whispered the spinster, "you told me that man was in New-York."

"So he has been for nearly two weeks. It seems he is back again to-night; aren't you glad?"

"No," grimly returned the old maid; "however, he will be too tired to speak, that is one comfort."

To her surprise, Mr. Rose was soon called upon for an address. He went up on the platform, but said we might have excused him, for he had been travelling since ten o'clock last night, and his head was all in a whirl. He then gave a most interesting account of his visit to New York and Saratoga. In the former place, he went with a friend to one of the worst streets in the city. On arriving and seeing great crowds of men, women and children in rags and dirt, his companion said to him, "Will you risk your life by passing through that street?" "*They're human!*" was Mr. Rose's reply; and, buttoning his coat more closely around him, he added, "I'll go it!" And he did. Such wretchedness, such fearfully dirty houses he had never witnessed in his life. On succeeding days, he walked through other streets of the city. His intention was to see how New York stood with regard to intemperance. But, during all his walks, he only saw two drunken men; one of whom was holding on to a wheel to steady himself. The people there drink lager beer. Mr. Rose was told by a chemist that since so much was drunk, it was now being manufactured from vile materials. Therefore, it was no gain to the people in a Temperance point of view. He then spoke of the time when lager beer was first introduced into Canada. It was said to be a Temperance drink, and he took a glass of it which affected his head for an hour afterwards. He was actually afraid that people might think him intoxicated. That one glass was sufficient to convince him that lager beer was not a drink for Temperance men, and he advised his audience to let it alone. It is needless to add that Mr. Rose never touched it again. He went on to speak of a Convention in Saratoga, where he, with some others, succeeded in getting a resolution passed, pledging the churches of his own

denomination to Total Abstinence. They had
never come out squarely for Temperance before
—were philosophical and indifferent about the
matter; but now Mr. Rose rejoiced in the fact.that
the reproach was rolled away. (" Oh isn't that
good !" whispered Hattie; " I am so glad that he
was doing Temperance work, out there—even
in a Church Convention, he did not forget it.")
Mr. Rose spoke of the *dissipation* of Saratoga.
Even the ladies would be up by six o'clock in the
morning, and without waiting to put on their
bonnets, would throw a shawl over their heads
and go off to drink—glasses of cold water from
the springs.   He told them that really he was a
Canadian and could not countenance such dissipation !   At first they thought him in earnest. A
large quantity of water was drank there, but very
little liquor.   Mr. Rose then went on to offer some
suggestions to the Executive Committee.   He advocated having more Temperance in our Saturday
night meetings, far more Temperance, because we
did not just come to have our ears tickled with
songs.   He then enumerated a number in the hall
who could speak, and was quite willing to allow

the ladies to take part. Referring to a song that had been sung ("Hearts of Oak,") he spoke of one of which it reminded him, which was common in Temperance meetings a number of years ago—

> "Cheer up, my lively boys,
> In spite of rum and cider,
> Cheer up, my lively boys,
> We'll sign the Pledge together."

The audience listened attentively and frequently applauded the eloquent speaker, who came down from the platform amid clapping of hands and stamping of feet. Mr. Walker, the chairman, fully agreed with the suggestions of Mr. Rose, and declared that "one earnest Temperance address would do more good than all the songs that could be sung from now until the Judgment Day."

Towards the close of the proceedings, a half-intoxicated man was desirous of saying a few words to the audience. The chairman mildly remarked that it was late, and it would be better to do so at another time.

"Let him speak!" said Mr. Rose, and the man went up on the platform. His address was very

short—the substance of it being, that "he had
not a cent to his name, to-night; and it was all
through drinking rum!" On coming down, Mr.
Rose told him to "sign the pledge" and he did so.

"Was it not a good meeting, Mrs. Harding?"
asked Hattie, in returning home with her friends.

"I pay very little attention to Temperance,"
answered Matilda, gravely; "but actually could
not help listening to Mr. Rose. There is something about that man that makes me feel ashamed
of myself. Don't ask me to come here again, Mrs.
Somerville, for, if I heard him speak often, I
should be compelled to give up my—well my *but-
terfly* kind of life, and try to do better for the future."

"Then, Matilda, you might be thankful to hear
him as often as possible!" earnestly replied Hattie.

Mrs. Harding made no reply. `

"Do you never go to Temperance meetings in
the West End?" asked Miss Wood.

"Oh, yes, but—"

"There is'nt a Mr. Rose in your Club!" emphatically remarked Hattie.

"No," answered Mrs. Harding with a sigh of
relief, "and I'm thankful for it."

CHAPTER II.

"IT'S raining, Hattie; surely you are not going out to-night."

"Of course I am, Aunt Fanny; and so are
you?"

"What have you got on your arm? Why,
my water-proof——"

"Yes, and here are your bonnet and rubbers;
I thought to save you the trouble of walking up
stairs," said Hattie, with a laugh.

"Indeed, how obliging you can be when it
suits your purpose!" exclaimed Miss Wood, at
once commencing to envelop herself in the big
water-proof cloak.

"We shall be late, Aunty Fanny ; let me put on your rubbers "

" No, I won't ;" and the old maid gave her niece a vigorous push. "You may black Edward Carswell's boots and welcome, if ever you get the chance, and Mr. Rose's into the bargain, for anything I care—not, but that I should pity those gentlemen, if they had to wear boots that had been in your hands !"

"Come, come, Aunt Fanny, do hurry yourself a little," said Mrs. Somerville, with a laugh; "there is Ronald at the door, now."

When the party arrived at the hall, there were only a few persons present. The piano accompanyist could not come until nine o'clock, and her substitute did not put in an appearance at all.

"We shall just be sent home," peevishly remarked Miss Wood ; "Ronald, do leave us for a moment and inquire what they are going to do."

Mr. McFarlane did so, but soon returned, and said, "Several of the officers thought that we must of necessity adjourn without opening the meeting at all, but Mr. Rose would not hear of sending the people away. Therefore it was pro-

posed, as the only way to retain them, that Mr.
Rose should kindly consent to speak for half an
hour or more, until Miss Boyd arrives."

" Oh, I'm so glad ; isn't it a happy thing that
we came !" said Hattie, and she rubbed her hands
for joy.

The old maid nervously fingered her water-
proof cloak and cast a furtive glance toward the
door. Mrs Somerville at once concluded that her
elderly relative was meditating flight, so she came
to the rescue by saying, " Aunt Fanny, I've just
found out the reason why you don't want to hear
Mr. Rose speak—you're actually afraid of being
convinced !"

That was quite sufficient ; the spinister leaned
back proudly against her seat and disdained to
make any reply.

In the meantime, Mr. Rose was inquiring good-
naturedly of the officers around him as to the subject of his address.

" Total Abstinence," promptly replied Mr.
Hassard.

It was intended to open the meeting without
singing, but Mr. Rose would not hear .of that

either, and insisted on having "All hail the power
of Jesus' name !" Those around doubted whether
it could be done without a musician ; so, in his
usual playful manner, Mr. Rose suggested that
they sing

> "How doth the little busy bee
> Improve each shining hour ;" etc.

or,

> "Let dogs delight to bark and bite,
> For God hath made them so ;
> Let bears and lions growl and fight,
> For 'tis their nature too."

Finally, as Mr. Rose insisted on opening the meeting with a hymn, they sang the one of his choice,

> "All hail the power of Jesus' name !
> Let angels prostrate fall ;
> Bring forth the royal diadem,
> And crown Him Lord of all."

After which, Mr. Rose asked "the friends" to
come to the front. Instead of going up on the
platform, as usual, he stood just below, leaning
against it, on a level with his audience, and told
them that he had been called upon to speak, the
only subject given him being that of Total Absti-

nence. But it was a very good subject. If there was a person present who regretted having signed the Pledge, Mr. Rose asked him to stand up. None complied ; so the speaker took it for granted that there was not one in the hall who was sorry for being a Total Abstainer. Some parties were present now, who were with us a year ago 'They had got among bad companions and fallen back ; but they were here to-night, and intended to try again. Mr. Rose impressed upon the reformed men how necessary it was for them to keep away from evil company. As no one could take fire in into his bosom and his clothes not be burned, nor any touch tar without being defiled, so it was impossible to associate with bad companions and not be injured thereby. He earnestly advised the reformed men to get down on their knees in the morning and ask God to help them and keep them from falling into temptation. " God helps those who help themselves ;" he said, and emphatically added, " *God will not help those who will not help themselves !* " He maintained that the Lord's Prayer was not correctly translated, for as it says " God never leads any man into temptation."

C

In speaking of the clergy, he evidently considered
them very deficient in their duty. "Intemperance is the greatest hindrance to the cause of
Christ," said Mr. Rose; "but do we hear many ministers preach against it from their pulpits, Sunday after Sunday?" He had no desire to say
anything against the clergy individually, for many
of them had given in their adhesion to the Temperance cause; but as a body, he thought they
should be more actively engaged in the good
work of persuading men to abstain from the
use of liquor as a drink. Mr. Rose also spoke
of sacramental wine and urged most strongly
that it should not be of an intoxicating nature.
There had been a marked change in this respect
of late years; for, even in Scotland, among the
Presbyterians, who are very conservative in their
opinions, there are churches which provide *two*
tables, one with the pure, unfermented wine, and
the other with "that which will knock a man
down!" (The audience laughed—they must have
been struck with the incongruity of the thing.)
He then went on to tell us of a reformed man
who had succeeded in keeping his pledge for

some time. One Sunday, he was in the church of which Mr. Rose is an office-bearer, and remained to the communion, as all are invited to do who wish. When the wine was passed, he inquired of one of the deacons if it were intoxicating. The person addressed did not know, and therefore came to Mr. Rose asking, "Is this wine intoxicating?"—"No, it's not!" replied Mr. Rose, but, the words were no sooner out of his mouth, than he almost fainted for fear there might be some mistake and the reformed man again fall away. The wine was all right at the previous communion season, but whether it had been changed and new had been procured, Mr. Rose was not sure. He was in misery for some minutes, until the wine came to him, when he at once found it was all right. ("Oh," said Hattie in a low voice, "what a pity that all the ministers in the city are not here to-night!") Mr. Rose went on to state that the money sent away for missions might be profitably employed in our own country among the heathen at our doors. The South Sea Islanders had the light of nature to guide them, and were, if any-

thing, in a better position than many in this country. Especially was it desirable to take the
gospel to the tavern-keepers! Mr. Rose then
related the touching story of the " Little Shoes."
A workman, who used to spend nearly all his
money at the tavern, saw a pretty pair of new
shoes on the landlady's baby. His own little
one was in her mother's arms, outside, on a
cold winter's night. It had neither shoes nor
socks. The man's heart smote him. He went
out, took his child and put its little cold feet under his coat. Though he had only a trifle of
money left, it was sufficient to buy shoes for the
baby and a loaf of bread. The next morning, he
went to work and brighter days dawned on his
family. When asked to account for his becoming
a total abstainer, the man would answer, " The
little shoes—they did it all ! " Mr. Rose went on
to quote the lines

> " Tell me I hate the bowl,—
>   Hate is a feeble word ;
> I loathe—abhor—my very soul
>   With strong disgust is stirr'd
> Whene'er I see, or hear, or tell,
> Of the dark beverage of hell ! "

"or those who traffic in it!" added Mr. Rose.
He then spoke of our future prospects and reminded us how disappointed Mr.——(a leading
hotel-keeper) would be if the Club went down.
He and others engaged in the liquor business en-
tertained great friendship for us, or *professed* to
do so—"but," continued Mr. Rose, "I don't believe them—*I don't believe them!*" This reform
movement had caused them to lose thousands of
dollars, which otherwise would have gone into
their tills, therefore it stood to reason that their
professions of friendship were not true. Mr. Rose
urged us all to work—to bring others to the meetings—and said "it would be a burning shame, if
the Club were allowed to go down."

Mr. Rose was heartily applauded, both during his
speech and at its close. Soon Miss Boyd came in,
and the concert proceeded as usual. A large number signed the Pledge. One, a dissipated-looking
person, was brought up by Mr. Rose, who stood
by him, and laid his white hand on the man's
shoulder as he added his name to the list of signatures.

"Aunt Fanny," said Mrs Somerville, "what a

happy thing it was we were there ! That was
the longest speech I have heard Mr. Rose make
—but, oh, didn't it seem short ? "

" Not to me, " growled the spinster; " but, I suppose that both yourself and Mr. McFarlane could
with pleasure have listened to him all night."

" Indeed we could," replied Ronald.

" Of course you endorse every word—that about
missions with the rest."

" There may be differences of opinion in that
respect," answered the Professor.   " You must remember, madam, that Canada is a young country
and not wealthy like Old England. Whether
our resources could not be applied with great advantage among our own heathen, is a subject that
requires careful consideration."

" Never think that Mr. Rose is against missions,
Aunt Fanny," said Mrs Somerville warmly. " I
was near the front, for a while, to-night, you
know ; and was so fortunate as to hear him read to
some one who sat just before me, hymn No 18 in
" Sacred Songs and Solos," commencing at the
second verse,—

" If you cannot cross the ocean,
 And the heathen lands explore,
You can find the heathen nearer,
 You can help them at your door.
If you cannot give your thousands,
 You can give the widow's mite ;
And the least you do for Jesus
 Will be precious in His sight.

" If you cannot speak like angels,
 If you cannot preach like Paul,
You can tell the love of Jesus,
 You can say He died for all.
If you cannot rouse the wicked
 With the Judgment's dread alarms,
You can lead the little children
 To the Saviour's waiting arms.

" If you cannot be the watchman,
 Standing high on Zion's wall,
Pointing out the path to Heaven,
 Offering life and peace to all ;
With your prayers and with your bounties
 You can do what Heaven demands ;
You can be like faithful Aaron,
 Holding up the prophet's hands.

" If among the older people
 You may not be apt to teach—

'Feed my lambs,' said Christ our Shepherd,
'Place the food within their reach.'
And it may be that the children,
You have led with trembling hand,
Will be found among your jewels,
When you reach the better land.

"Let none hear you idly saying,
'There is nothing I can do,'
While the souls of men are dying;
And the Master calls for you.
Take the task He gives you gladly,
Let His work your pleasure be ;
Answer quickly when He calleth,—
'Here am I, send me, send me !' "

"Aunt," said Hattie excitedly, "those words,
pronounced with such thrilling earnestness—
'Here am I, send *me*, send *me*!' will ring in my
ears for a month to come ! God has sent him of
a truth ; and, if ever there was a missionary,
Brother George Maclean Rose is one !"

CHAPTER III.

"THE GRAND LEVELLER."

"HATTIE, just leave me alone ; I'll go and get ready in a few minutes. Stop, Mr. Rose is not likely to speak again to-night, is he ? It was only last Saturday that they persuaded him to give that half-hour address."

Hattie shook her head and sorrowfully replied, " I'm afraid not. Three and four weeks have often elapsed between his short speeches, but since the Club has got so low, he has stuck to it all the more faithfully, and we have the pleasure of hearing his voice a little oftener than we otherwise would."

" Then it's not likely he will speak to-night ; so I'll go."

Which she accordingly did ; and was as much
annoyed as her two companions were delighted,
when the chairman called on " Brother Rose."

" Oh, it's too bad, " said the old maid ; " I have
not got over the effects of his last speech yet, (it's
just like you to laugh, Hattie, you're an illnatured
thing !) and to think of coming in for another
dose to-night ! "

" Cheer up, Aunt Fanny ; we shall all be the
better for it, " gleefully whispered Mrs. Somerville.

Mr. Rose complied with the request of the
chairman and went up on the platform to make
the closing appeal. He spoke of the short " Temperance talk" which had just been given by Brother More, in which the latter stated that he had
tried drinking for forty years, and had only been
a teetotaller for sixteen months, but was much
the better for his comparatively short abstinence.
Mr. Rose reminded the ladies of the influence they
possessed, and exhorted them to use it for good.
He was happy to see that the people had taken
his advice and brought their friends with them.
He told the women that if they had no one at

home with whom to leave their babies, they were to bring them to the hall rather than stay away. "We will look after them," said Mr. Rose; "I'll take care of half-a-dozen, myself!" He spoke of the hereditary influence of liquor and suggested that it would be well for us all to be on our guard, as we could not be sure of what our great grandfathers were in the habit of doing. He then earnestly appealed to his audience to come forward and sign the pledge, while the choir sang the closing hymn.

On reaching home, Miss Wood and her niece found Dr. Mays snugly ensconced on the sofa. He started up on their entrance and warmly embraced his daughter, remarking, "You are looking first rate, Hattie. Ronald is taking good care of you."

"Yes, and so am I," snapped Miss Wood; "but no one thinks of giving old maids any credit!"

"Oh, they'll take it themselves!" laughed the doctor.

The following day Mrs. Somerville pressed her father to accompany them to the Experience meeting.

" Yes, and I am going too," chimed in Miss Wood. " Happily for me, Mr. Rose is too busy with his Bible Class to take any part in it; when he does drop in, after Sunday School is over, the meeting is just closing, so that he cannot very well inflict his horrid Prohibitionist speeches upon us then."

"Aunt Fanny, you ought to be ashamed of yourself!"

"Indeed she ought, Hattie," said the doctor laughing. " Fan," he continued, " have you not got educated up to Prohibition yet—really, it is time you had!"

" Hold your tongue, Will," said the spinster angrily ; " I assure you it is from no lack of hearing enough about it;" and she cast a malignant glance at the picture of Mr. G. M. Rose, encircled with its wreath of ivy leaves.

" I like that photograph very much," observed Dr. Mays ; " Hattie was shewing it to me this morning. I have heard so many times about Mr. Rose, that I would like to hear him speak. Is there no chance of that pleasure this afternoon ?"

Mrs. Somerville mournfully shook her head.

" I'm afraid not, papa ; but come with us and I'll
so gladly shew him to you,—that is, if he is in
the hall at closing time, as is generally the case."

" What is he like, Hattie ? "

" Why, like that picture, father."

" That may be, my daughter ; but you cannot
always judge from a photograph."

" Well, what do you want to know ? " asked
Hattie, good naturedly.

" What a goose you are," said the old maid ;
" why not go on and describe him. Say he has
beautiful hair and so forth !"

" Very true, Aunt Fanny," coolly replied Hattie ; " you can do it better than I. Brother Rose
has beautiful, dark, golden-red hair, that's a fact.
Pray go on."

" I'll not do it," snapped Miss Wood ; " for you
will just take my words in earnest. You can describe him yourself."

" I scarcely know how," replied Hattie gravely.
" Brother Rose has deep blue eyes which seem to
look right through you, I believe he can read
your very thoughts ! "

" Indeed ! " said Miss Wood, " then, I'll sit a

few seats further back, in future, and give him a
wide berth. Just think what an unpleasant person he would be for a criminal to come in contact
with ! "

" Not if the criminal were penitent," answered
Mrs. Somerville; "for the better and holier a man
is, the less he is inclined to cast stones at others."

Miss Wood frowned and remarked in an ironical tone, " Mr. Rose is possessed of all the virtues
in the calendar ! "

" Do you think I'm going to dispute it ?" asked
Hattie, with a laugh.

" My niece, I would like to box your ears," angrily replied the spinster. " It is a comfort that
that man cannot speak to-day, at all events.
Come, it is time to get ready."

On arriving at the hall, Dr. Mays was surprised
at not finding a larger audience present. " The
Club has certainly gone down," he remarked.

" Yes, papa; but it is gaining all the time now.
Mr. G. M. Rose is the life of it. He stuck to the
Club through all its darkest days, or it would
have gone under long ago !"

More people came into the hall, in twos and

threes. Hattie touched her aunt's arm, saying, "There is one of Mr. Rose's Bible Class—they cannot be holding their school this afternoon. Oh, won't it be good if Mr. Rose comes early enough to speak ? Father will hear him then."

Her surmises proved correct. For some reason the Sabbath School had been held that morning, instead of in the afternoon, as usual.

A number of experiences were given of more or less interest. Mr. Halliday, in the course of his remarks, declared that "every man who drank liquor was a born fool." To that statement, Mr. Hassard took exception with some warmth. Mr. Halliday mildly replied that those who had reformed, could not help thinking of themselves in their drinking days as "fools." During Mr. Halliday's address Mr. Rose entered the hall, accompanied by his wife. He was especially requested to speak, by the chairman, and immediately complied. After expressing his pleasure at seeing so many present, he went on to say that he agreed with Mr. Halliday's remarks, and emphatically declared that every man who drank liquor was a fool. Mr. Rose spoke of the time when there

were no Teetotal societies. When they came into
existence, his father, who was a moderate drinker,
joined immediately, and remained a temperance man during the rest of his life. Mr. Rose
has three brothers and two sisters—all of them
teetotallers from their youth. He said that their
family had suffered as little from intemperance as
could well be, yet they had suffered, for some of
their relatives had fallen victims to the vice and
now filled drunkards' graves. What family could
not say the same ? Drink would overcome the
intellectual and educated as well as those who
were ignorant. " Drink is the grand leveller—in-
dulge in it and it will bring you down to the low-
est depths of degradation." In his remarks on
our social customs, he mentioned a public dinner given lately at which the Governor-General
was present. A leading Teetotaller occupied the
chair, to whom Mr. Rose remarked, " What a fix
they put us Temperance men in.—You will
look comical when you ask them to fill their
glasses !" "Rose, I'll not do it !" he earnestly
replied, and he kept his word. Those who
drank liquor, did so uninvited ; and many respon-

ded to the toasts in cold water. Mr. Rose expressed his surprise that people in general were so indifferent about the cause. He hoped the day would come when there would be a Temperance Society in every church. It would be well if the liquor traffic were put down two hundred years from now ; but we must work as though we expected it next week. We must work for those who will come after us. They will remember with gratitude our efforts to do away with the evil. Mr. Rose thought that it would take two hundred years to uproot the traffic entirely ; triumphantly adding, " and then the Millenium will come !" He concluded by urging upon those present the signing of the Temperance Pledge.

" Well, papa, aren't you glad you heard Mr. Rose ? He has not spoken in those Sunday meetings since last July, and this is the 13th of October; so you have reason to be thankful that you came with us to-day."

" There is no wonder you like him, my daughter ; he is thoroughly in earnest."

" Alas, far too much so for me !" exclaimed the spinster. " I don't admire those ultra-temperance

D

men at all ; they are crazy and fanatical. Now
it is quite useless to look so provoked, Hattie !
Mr. Rose need not be constantly poking Prohibition into us, and on a Sunday, too, of all days ! "

" Take care, Aunt Fanny; if I mistake not, you
will yet become a convert yourself."

Dr. Mays laughed.

" May be so," answered Miss Wood, in an unbe-
lieving tone; "but Mr. Rose will never convert me."

" Then I despair of anybody else doing it,"
replied Mrs. Somerville, gravely.

" My daughter," said the physician, " I was becoming cold in the cause myself—don't look so
horrified, child; your letters would probably have
prevented me from freezing to death—but I shall
be cold no longer, Hattie; Mr. Rose has given me
such a lesson that I shall never forget it ! "

" I am glad of that, sir," said Ronald ; "for
nearly all of us get discouraged sometimes."

" Does Mr. Rose ? "

" I don't think so, papa," quickly returned
Hattie. " You see he is different from everyone
else, and discouragements do not seem to affect him.
Mr. Rose just keeps his eye upon Christ and goes
straight ahead ! "

CHAPTER IV.

THE PROHIBITION "PLANK."

"WRITING to your father again, Hattie?
You always send him two letters a
week; and I often wonder what you can find
to say."

"Oh, I'm never at a loss, Aunt Fanny. Temperance is a good subject, you know."

"Doubtless you favour him with accounts of
Mr. Rose's speeches and so forth."

"Yes; and just now I was describing the
Women's Temperance Convention."

"What could you possibly find to interest him
in that?"

"Why, Miss Willard's lecture in the Baptist

church—some scraps of information about Mrs.
Youmans—"

" I don't like her; she is a Dunkinite."

" For shame, Aunt Fanny; everyone ought to
like her. Mrs. Youmans said that we must have
the pledge in one hand and a prohibitory law in
the other. She informed us, from personal obser-
vation, that there are children in Maine, who
never knew what a liquor license meant. Oh, is it
not a pity that our young ones in Canada are not
in such a state of blissful ignorance ?"

" No, "growled the spinster. " Did she say anything, Hattie, about Conservatives and Reformers ? "

" Mrs. Youmans does not intermeddle with politics, aunt. She said 'there is only one plank in
my platform and that's Prohibition !' "

"Not a word more; I've heard quite plenty.
Just go on with your letter, my niece, and hold
your tongue."

Mrs. Somerville laughed and at once began to
comply. Soon afterwards there was a light tap
at the study door and the Professor entered.

" Hattie," said the old maid, "this is too bad.

Be good enough to take yourself out of my den, and Ronald will speedily follow. This is Monday morning, and I really cannot make any progress while you two are going on with your ceaseless chatter."

The old maid was soon left in peace; she immediately arose and locked the door.

After some conversation with the Professor, Hattie suddenly remarked, " Ronald, did you ever have students come to you who were troubled with infidel and semi-infidel doubts ? "

" Yes, my dear, there were many such cases."

" How would you satisfy their minds about the apparent discrepancies in the Bible—such as the different accounts of the resurrection of Christ, etc. ? "

" Those students, who were honestly anxious to have their doubts solved, I would refer to some ' Harmony of the Gospels,' or a good commentary. Of course, I would explain, myself, by a simple illustration from every-day life, how easily such apparent discrepancies might arise. Students, who were Mr. Gregs on a small scale, I would treat in a different way."

"Ronald, please give me such an illustration. I asked Aunt Fanny a similar favour the other day, and she told me I was the most ignorant creature alive, and gave me Paley's 'Evidences' to study."

Ronald laughed. "Happily we have both learned to take your aunt's compliments for what they are worth." After thinking for a moment or two, he asked, "Let me see that letter to your father—you have mentioned the special concert of last Saturday night."

"Indeed I have!" indignantly returned Hattie, as she handed over the half-written letter.

Ronald took out his pocket diary and compared the two accounts.

Hattie saw his meaning and smiled. "We are independent witnesses," she remarked; "and I hope have both spoken the truth. Are there any discrepancies?"

"Yes, my dear; and persons living two thousand years after this would find great difficulty in reconciling our accounts. The majority of them would doubtless set down you or me as guilty of falsehood. Now, let me read aloud the ex-

tract from your letter. You say : ' I was thoroughly provoked, father, at the special concert of the
26th instant, and wished I had been near our
chairman, Mr. Walker, to have pulled his ears well
for him. He deserved it. So many times in that
position as he has been, too ! The cause was
shamefully neglected. He called for songs,—songs,
until we were tired of them ; but not until the
very last, when all the people were satiated and
anxious to get home, did he call upon the speaker
of the evening, Brother G. M. Rose. I suppose
other chairmen do stupid things sometimes, as
well as Mr. Walker. We want to do good and
get some new recruits. They are needed badly
enough, I'm sure. There was a fine, large audience, and I felt dreadfully aggravated that such
a splendid opportunity for impressing Temperance truths should be lost. Mr. Rose only spoke
a few words. He earnestly requested the young,
who had not commenced to drink, to join our
number; for prevention was better than cure.
Those who could not make up their minds that
night, were urged to come and sign the pledge on
the following Sabbath afternoon.'—So much for

your letter, Hattie; now I will read the short
entry in my diary. 'Saturday, Oct. 26th, 1878.
Special concert of Central Total Abstinence Club
held here (in Albert Hall) to-night. Rev. John
Potts in the chair. Admirably fitted for the posi
tion. Said in his opening speech that the liquor
traffic would die hard; the brewer, the distiller
would die hard; but,' he added earnestly, '*they
will die sometime and we will bury them so deep
that they shall never have a resurrection!*' "

Hattie smiled. "I understand now," she said,
"how easily discrepancies may arise. Some Mr.
Greg, living two thousand years hence and in a
different country, might say with perfect truth,
'If the chairman were Mr. Potts, he could not
have been Mr. Walker; and if the chairman were
Mr. Walker, he could not have been Mr. Potts.'"
Hattie laughingly continued, "The supposed Mr.
Greg would doubtless draw the following conclu-
sion, 'One of the accounts must necessarily be
untrue, and probably *both* may be regarded as un-
reliable !' "

"That is a fair specimen of Mr. Greg's mode of
reasoning, my dear," replied Ronald, with a smile.

" Persons, who wished to reconcile your letter
with my diary, might suggest the possibility of
having two chairmen at the same time, or consider one a deputy of the other. Should that explanation be deemed unlikely, others might suppose that, in some unaccountable way, the chairman might have had two names, one an alias or
something of the kind."

" Yes, Ronald," briskly rejoined Hattie; "and,
if perchance some indefatigable harmonizer managed to hit upon the true explanation, viz., that
Mr. Potts was unavoidably absent after the first
hour and Mr. Walker had to take his place, would
not objectors of the Mr. Greg stamp scout the
very idea of such a thing, and regard it as a
groundless supposition, gotten up expressly for
the occasion ?"

" Indeed they would, Hattie. You have read
Greg's ' Creed of Christendom,' I see."

" Yes ; not, however, from any sympathy with
the author. I merely wished to see what objections he could possibly bring against the Bible
from a scientific point of view."

" What is your opinion of him ? "

"Mr. Greg seems to me to treat the whole subject unfairly. He searches the Bible, not to learn the will of God, but to endeavour to overturn as much of it as possible. He pretends to do this sorrowfully; which reminds me of crocodile's tears, for I don't believe him. When he insists that this verse, that passage, or even a whole book of the Bible, is not to be depended on, it is evident to every unbiassed reader that 'the wish is father to the thought.'"

"Exactly so, Hattie; and, when students come to me in that spirit, I never try to convince them, for it would be useless, but simply refer them to two or three verses."

"On what subject—the doctrine of the Trinity?"

"Oh, no;" and the Professor smiled.

"Tell me the verses, please."

"I refer them to that beautiful passage in the tenth chapter of Luke—the only one which speaks of Jesus as 'rejoicing.' Our Saviour says, 'I thank Thee, O Father, Lord of Heaven and earth, that Thou hast hid these things from the wise and prudent, and hast revealed them unto babes : even

so, Father, for so it seemed good in Thy sight'
And, 'Verily I say unto you, Except ye be converted, and become as little children, ye shall not
enter into the kingdom of heaven.' Matthew
xviii. 3."

"Explain your meaning, please. I think I
know, but am not quite sure;" and Hattie's face
flushed.

"Well, when men come to the Bible in a
carping, criticising, fault-finding mood—what
makes you look so confused, my dear ; do you
know any such ?"

" Oh, yes, Ronald ; unfortunately they are not
hard to find."

"Those kind of people are not likely to dis-
cover either their sins or their Saviour. Very probably they have not the most distant idea that
they need Him at all. The truth is 'hidden'
from them. On the contrary, when men come,
not to sit in judgment on God's blessed Book, but
in a teachable, childlike spirit, to learn of Jesus,
their doubts and difficulties will vanish, and
they will be guided into all truth."

Hattie looked earnestly into the face of the

Professor. "Then, Ronald, such men are safe, I'm very glad. Christ will lead them, by slow degrees, it may be, but He will lead them to know Himself more perfectly, and they will be saved."

CHAPTER. V.

DON MOUNT.

"INVADING my den again, Hattie! I thought you contented yourself in the house on Friday nights. Of course Ronald is away; but I don't want to go out this evening, so there's an end of it."

"You live in the central part of the city, Aunt Fanny, and have no excuse."

"It is true that the Temperance and Albert halls are close at hand. For which are you bound to-night?"

"For neither."

"Then it's McMillan's! That is further away."

"Oh, no great distance," replied Hattie. "A dear little hall it is;" she continued, "with Prohibition painted on one side and Moral Suasion on the other. But I'm not going there to-night."

"Where then ?"

Hattie smiled mischievously. "Just over the Don, Aunt Fanny."

"Over the Don !" screamed the spinster ; "I'll not go."

"All right," calmly replied Mrs. Somerville. "Do not sit up for me, Aunt, for it will be late."

"You are a contrary, headstrong thing, " angrily exclaimed Miss Wood. "Do you suppose I shall let you go by yourself—no indeed ; bring me my bonnet and shawl ! "

During the whole way there, the spinster spoke not a word, much to Hattie's discomfort, who finally came to a stand-still before a plain, wooden building on the other side of the Don.

"Is this the place ? "

"Yes, Aunt Fanny."

"Well, it's the oldest, ugliest, most outlandish looking hall, that I ever saw in my life ! "

Hattie laughed.

"And how much longer are we to wait outside ? "

" Oh, just till some one comes to open the door and light up."

" It's too bad ; I shall get my death of cold standing here. You say it is a meeting to resuscitate a dead Division. Who are going to speak ? "

" Mr. G. M. Rose and——"

" That's enough," angrily interrupted Miss Wood. " What does it matter how old and ugly the hall may be ? Of course his presence will glorify it ! "

" I'm glad to be able to agree with you in that," replied Mrs. Somerville, calmly.

The hall proved to be better inside than out ; it was prettily decorated with evergreens and little flags.

Miss Wood kept looking anxiously around when she heard the door open. " I shall be agreeably disappointed if Mr. Rose does not come, " said she.

" Oh, I hope he will, " earnestly replied Hattie. " It is very evident he is needed out here at Don Mount. There he is now, and Mr. Daniel Rose. Isn't that good ? "

" Hold the Fort " was sung, and after a few re-

marks from Mr. Caswell, the chairman, the opening address was given by the Grand Worthy Patriarch, Bro. Millar.   He related several incidents,
which shewed the evils of intemperance, and spoke
of the progress of the Order of the Sons of Temperance in Canada.

Brother G. M. Rose was next called upon.   He
went up on the platform, and, with his usual eloquence and earnestness, delivered a stirring Temperance address.   In speaking of the organization
of the " Sons," he mentioned some incidents of his
own life, which were deeply interesting.   When
a boy of twelve years of age, he made up his mind
never to drink a drop of liquor, and then signed the
Pledge.   The Order of the Rechabites, which was
partly a benefit society, was in existence in the
part of Scotland where he resided, and though he
was a member of the Total Abstinence Society,
he also joined that Order.   Seeing one day in a
foreign newspaper an account of the Sons of Temperance and the good they were accomplishing in
the United States, Mr. Rose resolved that if ever
he crossed the Atlantic, he would become a Son
of Temperance.   At that time he had no idea of

the aggressive nature of the "Sons," and did not suppose this Order would ever reach Scotland. In the year 1851 he crossed to America, and on arriving at Montreal, inquired if the Sons of Temperance had an organization there. He was told that they had, and at once united himself with the "Howard Division" of that city. He then gave an account of the formation of the old Washingtonian Society, stating that a number of "jolly good fellows," as they called themselves, used to meet night after night at their favourite tavern. On such an occasion, one of them was so struck with the evil course he was pursuing, that he resolved to abandon it and never drink any more. He was laughed at by his companions; but when they saw the improvement that had taken place in his personal appearance and also in his home, they resolved to try the same plan. Thus the old Washingtonian movement was begun. It was a wave—much like the one that has just swept over our own land. After a while many who were at first enthusiastic in the work became indifferent, and the excitement began to wane. It was resolved, however, that the good

E

work should continue to go on, and sixteen Wash-
ingtonians met 29th Sept. 1842, in Teetotallers'
Hall, 71 Division Street, New York, and organized the first Division of the Order of the Sons of
Temperance. The new society seemed to meet
the requirements of the hour, and others were
speedily formed all through the Northern States.
In 1846 Mr. Philip S. White visited Montreal,
and during his stay a Division of the Sons was
formed, called "Montreal Division," which continued working for a short time. Mr. White
again visited Montreal in the fall of 1849, when
another Division, the "Howard Division" was organized, the one Mr. Rose joined when he first
came to this country, and which has been in
successful operation ever since. On the 21st of
June, 1848, the banner of the Order was first
unfurled in (then) Canada West, by Mr. George
Boyd, in the town of Brockville, on which was
inscribed in golden letters the motto of the
Order, "Love, Purity and Fidelity." The Brockville Division at its start only numbered eighteen
members, but since that time its influence has
been great, and at this moment the Order num-

bers in Ontario alone about fifteen thousand
members. Drinking men, continued Mr. Rose,
are always selfish; when they reformed, they
never thought of admitting their wives into
the Division-rooms. However the ladies became so
urgent, that the matter was discussed seriously for
some time, and the men finally resolved to admit
the women as visitors. "Such an act of condes-
cension!" said Mr. Rose; "Think of a man admitting his wife as a visitor! Why, when young,
those very men would stand at a gate for two
hours, on a cold winter's night, (as I've done myself) waiting for a girl to come out!" So the
ladies came in as visitors, but were soon dissatis-
fied and claimed full rights with their brethren.
It was a long while, however, before they got
them; but they succeeded at last. He spoke highly of the Order, and said that many of our public men had received their training in the Division
room. Sir John A. Macdonald was once a Son
of Temperance. Mr. Rose had the pleasure of
hearing the Hon. Mr. Tilley declare, in the Dominion Parliament, that, had it not been for the
education he received in the Division-room, he

would never have occupied his present position
on the floor of the House. He entered the Division at St. John, New Brunswick, a simple country lad ; the members welcomed him, and the
training he received there made him what he is.
Brother Tilley stood true to his Temperance
principles, even when appointed Lieutenant-
Governor. No intoxicating liquor was offered at
the table of the Government House while he was
the occupant; and, now that he is in Parliament
again, he is still faithful to the cause. Mr. Rose
spoke of the class-distinctions of the mother-
country and stated how difficult it was for the
sons of working-men to attain to places of honour
and position. In Canada, things were very different, and poor men's sons had an equal chance with
the rich. He encouraged the youths before him
with the assurance that some day they might
become Lieutenant-Governors. Mr. Rose stated
that a few of those who had originated the Order
were still alive. He had stood with them on
New York platforms—fine, grand looking old
men they were, with long, white beards. All
other secret Teetotal Societies had branched off

from the Sons of Temperance. The latter were
not jealous of either their children or grand-
children. He beautifully represented the various organizations as regiments in the Temperance army, and appealed to the people of Don
Mount to form a "company" and thus fall into
line! In speaking of the habits of obedience to
which children are trained in Scotland, he said
that the father would never think of allowing
his sons and daughters to take their meals with
him until they become a certain age ; but, in
this country, as soon as the baby could sit
up in its high chair, it was seated at the table.
His father would have frowned at such a thing
as his boys and girls taking their places beside him. Mr. Rose would not like his children
to regard him in that way ; still, it was possible
to occasionally wish for the old times, for instance,
when the little ones were determined to crawl
upon the table, just when you were desirous of
taking a quiet cup of tea! But, Mr. Rose added
in a playful tone, the discipline had done Bro. Millar and himself good; for it had taught them
obedience and enabled them "to take snubbing

meekly!" ("Oh, I don't believe it!" said Miss
Wood, " Mr. Rose doesn't look as though he would
ever take anything of the kind meekly—not he,
indeed!") Towards the close of the address, some
roughs who were sitting near the door arose to
leave. "Are you going away, young men?"
asked Mr. Rose kindly. "Are you tired?"
"Yes," said one of the band.

"You're not very enthusiastic," coolly returned
Mr. Rose, with a touch of sarcasm in his tone,
which none knows better than he how to apply.

Another of the lads, who was evidently
ashamed of the rudeness of his companion, remarked, "We belong to the Rine."

Miss Wood scowled horribly at the retreating
forms, and muttered, "Shame upon them; they
are a disgrace to the name of moral suasionsts."

After some further remarks, Mr. Rose came
down from the platform, and a short address
was given by his brother, Mr. Daniel Rose, who
related an incident about walking on St. James
street, Montreal, along with a son of a late member of Parliament. They passed a poor, ragged
and disreputable looking individual on the side-

walk. The young man looked after him and observed, that that poor, miserable drunkard went to school with him and had as good prospects in life as anyone in Montreal. He then said with bitterness, that came from his heart, " d—m drink !" This same young man lies in a drunkard's grave. Strong drink had already a · mastering hand over him, and his position in society did not save him from the destroyer. Mr. John McMillan also followed in a short address ; after which a conversation took place as to the best means of resuscitating the Division, and then the meeting adjourned.

" Eleven o'clock," said the spinster, on reaching her home ; " Well, I might have expected it, having to walk all that distance. Now, be off to bed, Hattie, or you will be late for breakfast."

"I'm going to write to father, while those speeches are fresh in my mind."

" You had better not," growled Miss Wood, " or I shall wake you at five o'clock to-morrow, instead of six ; and mind you don't go to sleep again."

Mrs. Somerville laughed. Her aunt's warning

went in at one car and out at the other, as. was
too frequently the case.

On the following day, the spinster was awakened by a gentle tap at her door and a merry
voice outside, exclaiming, " Five o'clock, Aunt
Fanny ; aren't you going to get up ? "

Miss Wood was wide awake in an instant.
" Come in, Hattie ; are you sick ? "

" Oh, no ; I could not sleep—never can, when
I am excited."

" How far did you get on in your letter last
night ?"

" To the end of the address of Brother G. M.
Rose. Oh, Aunt Fanny, did he not speak grandly !
How utterly impossible it is to do justice to his
remarks in any crude report."

" I presume it would, and am not going to
try," coldly returned the old maid.

" I hope you will go to sleep again, Aunt
Fanny ; I only awoke you from mischief."

" How is it possible for me to close my eyes for
a minute, while you are rampaging about the
house ? "

" Oh, I'll be quiet ; that letter will keep me

busy for an hour to come. Good night, or morning, rather," and Mrs. Somerville departed.

The spinster turned over, and in five minutes was fast asleep again.

Hattie entered her own room, read over her letter, and uttered a sigh of despair. " I don't believe Mr. Rose could write them out himself!" she said. " No one could do justice to his fiery, impromptu addresses, unless indeed it be the recording angel!"

When Miss Wood met her niece at the breakfast table, she inquired, " What did you think of the conduct of those young men last night?"

"It was shameful, Aunt Fanny. Tired indeed! I'm afraid Mr. Rose would be tired when he got home last night. Those roughs may be members of a Rine Club; but none of them are worthy to be Sons of Temperance, which is altogether a superior and more far-reaching organization. They missed some of the speeches by going out; but I am glad they heard nearly all of Mr. Rose's address, which cannot fail to benefit them afterwards, whatever it might do at the time. The Bible says, " Cast thy bread upon the

waters, for thou shalt find it after many days,"
and, Aunt Fanny, those very young men, who be-
haved so ill, will yet live to see the day when they
will thank God that He ever sent Brother George
Maclean Rose to help to resuscitate the Division
at Don Mount."

CHAPTER VI.

BUSINESS MEN.

"I'M glad to see you back, Ronald," said Miss Wood; " now be kind enough to look after Hattie, yourself. She actually dragged me over the Don last night to attend a Division meeting."

" Why did you go, ma'am ? "

" What a question to ask ! You know (or will soon find out, to your sorrow) that my niece is the most contrary creature you will meet in a day's march. Now, Hattie, you should not laugh, when you ought to feel very much ashamed. I am just warning Mr. McFarlane in time what to expect."

" Thank you, Aunt Fanny ! It will save me the trouble of telling him myself."

"How honest and honourable you can be, to be sure!" scornfully returned the spinster. "Now, I'm going to my study; you can entertain Mr. McFarlane with an account of the meeting last night."

"All right, aunt, I will."

In the afternoon, the party went to visit Mr. and Mrs. T. Harding, who lived in the West End. Ronald found an old school-mate there, whom he had not seen for years. His name was George Thorne. The conversation turned to former times.

"Oh, yes, old fellow," said Tom; "your father gave you a fine start; but mine had a large family and could not afford to do it. He gave us a good education, and then we had to fight our own way through the world. That gold watch was the only valuable thing he ever bought for me; and George I cannot bear to look on it even now!"

"Why not?" inquired his former room-mate, in surprise.

"Because I sold my Temperance principles, and bought that watch with a glass of wine."

"But, Tom," remonstrated his wife, "there are

plenty of Temperance people, who take liquor as a medicine."

"Then they're a disgrace to the cause, Matilda!" indignantly returned Hattie.

"You need not talk—it was your father who gave Tom that glass of wine."

"It was a very wicked thing, whoever did it," replied Mrs. Somerville, with reddening cheeks. "Father would not do so, now; he has been a total abstainer for many years."

"It was my own fault," answered Tom. "I had not only signed the Pledge, but faithfully promised Giovanni never to drink a drop of liquor in sickness or in health. Dr. Mays urged me to take it, if I wished to get well before the holidays—I thought of that promised watch and reluctantly drank the wine. I cannot bear to see it," added Tom, bitterly, "for it continually reminds me that I sacrificed principle and broke my word of honour for a glittering bauble."

Matilda laughed. "You are the most uncomfortably conscientious man I ever knew," she said. "It is a marvel to me, how you have got on so well in business, with such puritanical

views. I suppose you would sacrifice every cent
you own rather than do a dishonourable thing ! "

" Yes."

" Well, *I* wouldn't ! " laughingly returned Mrs.
Harding.

" Oh, Matilda, I'm ashamed of you ! " exclaimed
Hattie, " I'm really afraid that Mr. Rose's speech
did not do you any good after all."

" Good ! It has made me feel horridly uncomfortable ever since."

" I'm very glad to hear it," said her husband ;
" I'll take you to hear him again. Is he likely to
speak to-night ? "

" I hope so," replied Mrs. Somerville ; " for he
only said a few words at the special concert last
Saturday. Mr. Walker is a good fellow enough
but he made a sad mistake in keeping the best
part of the entertainment—viz., the speech of Bro.
G. M. Rose—until the close, when all the people
were weary."

" Was it not done from some evil motive ? " asked
the spinster.

" Oh, no," replied Hattie, with a laugh. " Do
not accuse Mr. Walker of anything of that kind.

When Mr. Rose wished to resign the office of Treasurer, Mr. Walker remarked most truthfully that "we should have to hunt high and low before we could find such another!" Our worthy first vice-president takes a great interest in Temperance matters, especially those that pertain to the Club. And I am sure there is not a member among us who would wish the shadow of a slight to fall upon our noble and kind hearted Treasurer—Brother G. M. Rose."

"Of course not," replied Tom; "I am glad you mentioned him. There is a business man for you! Matilda reflected on such of us as are engaged in money-making pursuits, as if we would sacrifice principle for wealth, but look at Mr. G. M. Rose! He is the President of two large publishing firms and has any amount of business on his hands, but he is the very soul of honour."

"Of course," earnestly replied Hattie. "Mr. Rose carries his religion into everything, and is just as much a Christian in his office as when he is at church taking the sacrament!"

"I'll not dispute it," said Matilda gravely; "but I do not believe there is one man in a thousand who is like Mr. Rose!"

" It is a marvel to me how he can find time for such a quantity of Temperance work," observed Ronald. " With him preaching and practice certainly go hand in hand."

"He does no more than his duty," coldly returned Miss Wood ; " and I am really aggravated because you all will persist in considering him the height of perfection."

CHAPTER VII.

" SUBSTITUTION."

THE meeting of the Central Club was held on that night, in the small hall, the larger one being otherwise occupied: Mr. Hassard was in the chair, and particularly requested an address from Brother Rose, who responded with his usual eloquence. He alluded to a sad case, which had been mentioned by the chairman; it was that of a father who had spent all his money for liquor and gone off leaving his wife destitute and little ones starving. They had not tasted food that day; and there was none in the house for Sunday. Mr. Rose denounced liquor as the cause of such unnatural conduct. He said that our legislators did not go as earnestly for the Tem-

F

perance cause as we would wish, and reminded
working men of the power they possessed.
They could compel our law-makers to grant their
demands. " I am the son of a working-man myself," added Mr. Rose. In speaking of those who
had already become addicted to the evil habit of
drinking, he said " God pity them! We will do
all in our power to help them," but, at the same
time strenuously urged that the young be taught
from their childhood to become total abstainers
and " when they were old they would never depart from it." It was impossible to controvert
the principles on which the Club was established.
" I defy anyone to stand up in this hall and declare that intoxicating liquors are good as a drink."
Mr. Rose added that many of us were prepared
to go further and maintain that they were not
good as a medicine. He blamed the doctors for
making drunkards by pandering to the vicious
desires of their patients and prescribing liquors.
Mr. Rose had not found it necessary to take liquor as a medicine for fifty years. (" I did not
think he had lived in the world so long," muttered Miss Wood to her niece.) Mr. Rose went

on to urge that Temperance be taught in schools, and severely reproved the teachers for being so indifferent in the matter. He strongly advised the introduction of Temperance lesson books ; and declared that there were some in the hall who knew more about that important subject than the Minister of Education himself.

"Tom," said Mrs. Harding, when the meeting was over, "I do wish that Mr. Rose had a grain or two of selfishness in his nature! He need not try to make us all as good as himself, for he will never succeed. He would actually make us believe that every one, *every one*, has a work to do."

" Matilda, does not your own conscience tell you that Mr. Rose is right ! "

"Yes," angrily replied Mrs. Harding; " but I'll not give in; and had I a hundred consciences, I would fight against them all."

" My dear, some day you will be sorry for saying such a wicked thing."

Matilda was silent; she was half afraid of it herself.

When Miss Wood arrived at her home, she

looked keenly at her niece and inquired, " What
is the matter ? "

Mrs. Somerville made no reply.

" Did you not enjoy Mr. Rose's speech? "

· " No, Aunt Fanny," mournfully answered Hattie, " he hit me too hard for that."

The spinster laughed aloud. " Indeed, I am
delighted to hear it—perfectly delighted ! "

There was no response, and Miss Wood mali- ·
ciously continued, "you look as though you were
going to cry, Hattie ! "

" Oh, no, Aunt Fanny. That would not do
any good. I might cry for a week, but tears
would never wash out the past."

The old maid became serious in an instant.
" Sit down, my niece ;" she said, " and tell me
what troubled you ? "

" Mr. Rose spoke of teachers——"

"Oh, yes ; so he did. And now, I call to mind
that many years ago, your father, (the foolish
man) consented to let you try school-teaching for
a few months, never dreaming that his contrary
daughter would go out in the bush and have for
scholars the rough children of shantymen and so
forth."

Mrs. Somerville smiled sadly as she recalled to mind the log houses, the vast, lone woods, and the rough but kind hearted children who had been under her care. The sharp voice of the spinster broke in upon her reverie, " Well, how much Temperance did you teach them ? "

" None at all."

" None at all ! You may well look troubled. So much as they needed it—no Sunday-school —no church, except an occasional service in your school-house—and many of them surrounded with bad influences into the bargain. You never warned them against the very sin that would be apt to overcome them : what could you be thinking about ? "

" I don't know, Aunt Fanny," returned Mrs. Somerville, mournfully. " There was no Temperance Society within reach, and it never struck me that I could work in such a place, single-handed. Many of the children had rough parents, and knew more of fighting and swearing than of the Bible. I taught them about Christ and the way of salvation ; but Temperance never entered my head. Liquor will be more apt to keep them

from the Saviour than everything else put together, and I have not uttered a word of warning against it.   Aunt Fanny, if those boys become drunkards, will they not be justified in
blaming me ? "

Miss Wood was silent ; she really felt sorry for
her niece. " Hattie," she asked at length, " is
there no way of remedying it now ?   Send them
some tracts."

" Aunt Fanny, I sent them Temperance papers,
books and tracts, long ago, and chromo pledge-
cards, too.   But doing one's best for the future,
does not wash out the past. What a blessing
there is *something* that will ! " Hattie arose as she
spoke and took a loose slip of paper out of her
scrap-book.

" What is that ? " inquired the spinster.

"The report in the *Globe* of the Rev. Joseph
Cook's lecture, last Thursday night."

" Read that part of it about substitution," said
Miss Wood, who was anxious to comfort her niece.

Mrs. Somerville read aloud, as follows : " We
cannot go hence in peace unless we are harmonized with our environment. Our environment

is made up of God, of the plan of our own natures, and of our record in the past, and therefore
we must be harmonized with God in conscience
and our record, or, in the very nature of things,
there can be no peace for us. There are three things
from which we cannot escape, our own natures,
God, and our record. * * * The unchangeable past
is a part of our environment. We must be harmonized with it. Am I harmonized with it when
I have reformed? There is an unchangeable record of my sin in the past. I have learned to hate
that sin, but ought the record of it to be treated
precisely as though it never had been? Here is a
deserter. Here is a soldier who never deserted.
The deserter comes back. He is ready to re-enlist.
Ought he to be treated just like the soldier that
never deserted! He ought to be treated differently, and God always does what He ought to do.
Therefore I feel an unrest as to this record in the
past, even after I have reformed. * * * I know
not what can be made clear from human history,
if it is not certain that in the absence of a deliverer
and of an expiation, man forebodes punish-
ment. That is the way we are made, and even

after we have reformed, human nature acts in this
manner.   The greatest saints, in the absence of
expiation, or when they have known nothing
of it, have had this foreboding, and in all ages
have had it.   The record of desertion behind a
man makes his past permanently different from
that of a man who has never deserted.   That past
which was an effect becomes a cause, and will per-
petually produce appropriate effects of foreboding
unless God's hand, as a screen, be let down between
us and it, and between His face and that black,
irreversible past.   I know I need such a screen.
But from mere reason I cannot prove that such a
screen has been provided for me.   Revelation says
*an atonement has been made.   That key turns in
the lock of human nature ; that fits the wards of
this foreboding.   That washes Lady Macbeth's red
right hand.** * *   Lady Macbeth, pacing up and
down, should be kept there forever to illustrate, in
the forefront of literature, and to all time, one of
the greatest of religious truths ; ' Out, accursed
spot.   All the perfumes of Arabia would not sweet-
en this little hand.' * * * There is nothing shadowy,
nothing uncertain about the fact that Lady Mac-

beth's hand is red; or the fact that she would like to wash it ; or the fact that she cannot. Who can ? Not Plato, not Socrates, not Gœthe, not Strauss, not Emerson—*only Christianity can wash Lady Macbeth's red right hand*."

" Very true, Hattie. I wish you had heard the whole lecture."

"So do I. Aunt Fanny, have you a Wesleyan hymn-book. Mine is at Roseville."

"Yes, half a dozen of them. What is it you want ?"

"That hymn which so beautifully speaks of Christ as our Surety. 'All ye that pass by,' etc."

" Oh, for shame, my niece. You knew that when a child. Surely you have not forgotten it now."

" I cannot remember it all."

"Go on, and I'll help you."

Hattie commenced as follows :—

CHRIST OUR SACRIFICE.

" All ye that pass by,
To Jesus draw nigh :
To you is it nothing that Jesus should die ?
Your ransom and peace,
Your surety He is ;
Come, see if there ever was sorrow like His.

For what you have done,
His blood must atone ;
The Father hath punished for you His dear Son.
The Lord, in the day
Of his anger, did lay
Your sins on the Lamb ; and He bore them away."

" I forget what comes next, Aunt Fanny."
Miss Wood immediately went on,

" He answered for all
O, come at His call,
And low at His cross with astonishment fall.
But lift up your eyes
At Jesus' cries :
Impassive, He suffers ; immortal, He dies.

" He dies to atone
For sins not His own ;
Your debt He hath paid, and your work He hath done.
Ye all may receive
The peace He did leave,
Who made intercession, ' My Father, forgive ! ' "

" Now, my niece, you surely remember the
rest."

Hattie smiled. " Yes, Aunt Fanny, I do ; and
what is more, believe it with all my heart."

" Then, go on."

" If you wish it," and Hattie proceeded,

" For you and for me
   He prayed on the tree ;
The prayer is accepted, the sinner is free,
    That sinner am I,
    Who on Jesus rely,
And come for the pardon God cannot deny.

" My pardon I claim
   For a sinner I am ;
A sinner believing in Jesus's name.
    He purchased the grace
    Which now I embrace ;
O Father, Thou knowest He died in my place.

" His death is my plea ;
   My Advocate see,
And hear the blood speak that hath answered for me.
    Acquitted I was
    When He bled on the cross ;
And by losing His life He hath carried my cause."

" Mr. Greg thinks the doctrine of substitution a most vicious one, my niece. Now, would you be guilty of the same neglect of duty again, because you could be forgiven ? "

" No, indeed Aunt Fanny. Those who love Christ, surely, *surely*, will not wilfully grieve Him."

" That is just what I think myself."

Seeing that her niece was somewhat comforted, the old maid could not refrain from remarking in an ironical tone. "You still like Mr. Rose, I hope!"

Hattie looked up in surprise. "Indeed I do," she answered warmly, "more than ever."

"You have not even spoken to him," said Miss Wood, "and I can assure you from experience, that many people of whom you think very highly, are far from being as perfect as you suppose, when you become personally acquainted with them. Do not forget that 'distance lends enchantment to the view.'"

"That is unfortunately too true in many cases; but it is all nonsense so far as he is concerned. Those who know Mr. Rose the best, are the very ones who love and esteem him the most."

"It is utterly useless to talk to you. I have not the slightest wish for even a distant acquaintance with him or any other fanatical Prohibitionist; but if you were so happy as to possess his friendship, you would not exchange it for all Canada—now, would you ? "

" No indeed, Aunt Fanny," returned Hattie, indignantly; " do you suppose the friendship of such a man as Mr. G. M. Rose is to be bought or sold? I am convinced that its 'happy possessors,' as you call them, would not exchange it for all the gold in the world."

"Nor Edward Carswell's either, I presume. Well, my niece, you won't hear of marrying Mr. McFarlane just yet; but, when you do, I advise you to go over to Maine on your wedding tour."

"Oh, we are, Aunt Fanny. Ronald has promised to stop a week or two in Portland; and it will not be my fault if I do not catch a glimpse of Neal Dow."

The spinster waited to hear no more, but at once left the room.

"Good-night, Aunt Fanny!" called her niece.

There was no reply.

CHAPTER VIII.

THE IDEAL FULFILLED.

"HATTIE," said Miss Wood, one day, "you are very close-mouthed about what takes place at Divisions. I can only form a poor idea, not being a member, and consequently forbidden to attend any except open meetings. Honestly, now, which did you enjoy the most, the last special concert of the Club, or the meeting of the Sons of Temperance at Don Mount last Friday?"

"The meeting at Don Mount," promptly replied Mrs. Somerville.

"Knowing what a taste you have, I am not greatly surprised. You can sit for a whole evening listening to speeches about the cause, but cannot appreciate music."

"Yes, I can; there are songs that——"

" Oh, of course, *Temperance*—you have neither heart nor soul for anything else ! "

" Aunt Fanny, that is not true."

" I know whether it's true or not ! " scornfully returned the spinster. " What is the initiation service like ? " she continued.

"Very beautiful, solemn and impressive. Something the same as installation. You must remember seeing Brother G. M. Rose install the officers of Rechab Division."

" Yes, I was much pleased with the service ; but not with the gentleman who performed it. Now scowl, Hattie, do ! When the business part of the ordinary Division meeting is over, do they have a good programme ? "

" Yes, they are generally very interesting. At Crystal Fountain Division we have plenty of music ; among others, Mr. Stark sings his Scotch songs so admirably that you would wish you were Scotch, Aunt Fanny ! "

" I don't believe it ! "

" Mr. Dilworth gives us good recitations ; Mr. Daniel Rose is always ready with some interesting and instructive reading ; and it is needless to add, that Mr. G. M. Rose, who is the moving spirit in the Division—nay, I might go further, and say the very life of it—contributes his full share towards making the meetings both pleasant and profitable. You know how beautifully he can read and recite ; and, as for delivering Temperance addresses I defy you to find his equal ! "

" That is all very well. Crystal Fountain has the name of being the best Division in the city—"

" In the Dominion !" interrupted Hattie, with a laugh.

" Have it your own way—in the Dominion ; but, as for making the meetings interesting, that would be hard to do, when the Division was small, like Rechab for instance."

" Not a bit of it, if the members are really in earnest and possess some brains. One of the most interesting meetings I ever attended was at Rechab Division, which though small as regards numbers, cannot well be beaten in point of pluck."

" Describe it, please. Surely the entertainment part is not a secret."

" Oh, no ; I presume not. Mr. Duncan gave a

very interesting and instructive lecture on poetry;
he explained the various kinds, read several
extracts, and called on Mr. Robert McConkey,
who sings well, to illustrate it by a song or two.
When he was in the middle of his lecture, Mr. G.
M. Rose came in, as a visitor, you know. Of
course, he was asked to speak, and very kindly
complied, entertaining the Division with a number of poems and snatches of poems, by way of il-
lustrating Mr. Duncan's lecture. Had you been
there, I am sure you would have enjoyed it un-
commonly, Aunt Fanny."

"It is quite likely I should; but, really, their
principles are such that I cannot unite with them
for they evidently go for the legal abolition of the
liquor-traffic. There is no Society in which I
could feel at home except those moral suasion
clubs."

Hattie laughed. "You are not always at home
in them."

"No," bitterly returned the spinster, "not when
they get a Prohibitionist, like that precious Mr.
Rose, on the platform."

"You say very truly," warmly replied her niece,

G

"Mr. Rose *is* precious! There is not another man in Canada, who has done such noble service for the cause."

"Hattie?"

"Well—"

"I never thought of it before—" and the old maid laughed long and heartily.

"Whatever is the matter?" inquired Mrs. Sommerville in surprise.

"Your ideal!"

Hattie saw at once her aunt's meaning, and she nodded and smiled.

"Strange that it never entered my head before," said the spinster. "Your ideal of a model Temperance man was one that I did not suppose could be realized."

"Nor I—but it has!" triumphantly exclaimed Hattie.

"You were far from easy to satisfy, my niece, that is a fact. No half and half character—very earnest in one branch of Temperance work, but cold in all the others—would satisfy you. Your ideal was a zealous moral suasionist combined with a thorough out and out Prohibitionist. No reformed drunkard; but a life-long Temperance man, hating liquor—yes, and (shame upon you) those who deal in it. Not one who *professes* both moral suasion and Prohibition, and then, when the testing time comes, votes away his principles for party; but one who is true as steel, whose motto is 'The ballot for Temperance,' who never casts anything but a Prohibition vote. My dear niece, at last you have discovered a man, in whom all those varied *excellences* meet—a man who comes up to your almost imposssible standard, and I congratulate you most heartily that your outlandish, fanatical ideal is completely fulfilled in that 'precious' Mr George Maclean Rose!"

CHAPTER. IX.

SEED-SOWING.

"HATTIE has sent us two tickets for the special concert, to-night, Tom ; and, in the accompaning note, she says that Mr. Rose is expected to speak, doubtless intending to charm us West-enders with his talismanic name."

"I shall certainly go, Matilda, if he is advertised to speak ; and so will you."

It was the evening of the 23rd November. The weather being cool, the hall was so crowded that more seats had to be brought in to accommodate the audience. A first-class entertainment had been provided for them, which they evidently enjoyed.

"It is all very good, so far," whispered Miss

Wood to her niece, " but the worst is yet to
come;" and she glanced at the platform, where
several gentlemen were sitting beside the chairman.

" Mr. Rose won't speak, he is shaking his
head," said Hattie. " Oh, I hope Mr. Handford
will not take his refusal ! "

The chairman explained to the audience that Mr.
Rose did not feel disposed to speak to-night, but
he called upon him all the same.

Mr. Rose came forward, and stated that, having
been away at Ottawa, he had not noticed until
this morning that his name was on the programme.
He referred to a reading just given by Mr. Handford, entitled " The Northern Farmer," by Tenny-
son, which represented a Yorkshireman insisting
that his son should have an eye to " property " in
his choice of a wife. Mr. Rose differed altogether
from the farmer, and advised his audience to marry
for love. " I married for love myself and worked
for 'siller,' as the Scotch call it." There had been
a discussion in the papers lately about the matrimonial question, and how one could live on $800 a
year. He began life on $525 a year and got on

well. "As for you, young ladies, many of you might have been married now, had you acted right. But you have not acted right." He referred to patriarchal times—how Noah planted a vineyard as soon as he came out of the ark—and said that if Mrs. Noah had put her foot down and resolutely refused to allow liquor to be used by her family, how much evil would have been prevented. He urged young ladies to have nothing to do with young men that drank liquor. Drink was the cause of wretched homes; that was the reason why men could not get along in married life. A man who was given to drink would not be happy in matrimonial relations. How many in his audience had $800 a year; and yet they had raised their children respectably, and it was easy to do it when drink was not indulged in. Mr. Rose was much pleased to see so many present. The well-dressed people before him made him feel that the Club was doing a good work There had been prophets who declared we could not accomplish any of the things we had already done. We were the people to carry on this movement; the workingmen of the city and the work-

ing-women too, were, under God, the instrument-
alities of building up this Club. The said Club,
however, was only doing one part of the work.
We did not have much about Prohibition spoken
here; but it was expected that in January, there
would be a grand Convention of Temperance men
in Toronto, who would talk Prohibition and nothing else. This work would go on until even
the Marquis of Lorne would have to give up his
Scotch whisky. Mr. Rose mentioned that there
were two persons present, who were members
when the Club was first organized and they were
not in a nice condition to-night. Some fiend had
tempted them and they had fallen away. Mr.
Rose emphatically added, " If a man tempts me
to do wrong I believe in knocking him down !"
(The chairman smiled broadly.) The speaker
went on to state that he had spoken before of a
poor, degraded drunkard whom he had picked up.
Mr. Rose forced him into a cab, took him to a
Temperance meeting and compelled him to sign
the pledge. That was some time ago. The man
stood firm, and when Mr. Rose left that city, he paid
the reformed drunkard's dues for a year or two in

advance, because the latter was careless and indifferent about attending Temperance meetings, and might have been suspended by the Division for non-payment. Some time afterwards the man was going to visit a friend in New York, who Mr. Rose knew was in the habit of pressing liquor on everybody, and moreover was so fond of it himself that he would even have made the devil drink, that is, if the devil would do so foolish a thing. So, in passing through Toronto, on his way to the States, of course the reformed man called to see Mr. Rose. Knowing well the danger to which he would be subjected, Mr. Rose took him into his private office and warned him of the same. The man who would tempt him to drink was not his friend, but his enemy; and if this person, in New York, urged liquor upon him, "knock him down!" said Mr. Rose. The reformed man maintained his Pledge inviolate; he did not fall, though there were some who in similar circumstances would have done so. Many had not the power to stand when temptation came in their way. Mr. Rose commended one of the leading doctors in England, because he would not pre-

scribe for his patients until they became total abstainers. He wished our Toronto doctors were of
the same stamp. We should then have more
Temperance men than at present. The ministers
also ("with all respect to our chairman," added
Mr. Rose) had a duty to perform. If they made
it a rule that none but those who had signed the
Pledge should be members of the church, the
number of total abstainers would be greatly increased. Mr. Rose stated that he was a Reformer,
a Clear Grit ; his friend Dilworth down there
was a Conservative ; but the time was coming in
which they would have to give up their Gritism
and Conservatism and go in for Temperance and
Temperance alone !

The spinster listened to the clapping of hands
and stamping of feet with evident dissatisfaction.

" I cannot see how it is that Mr. Rose carries
his audience with him so completely;" she
peevishly remarked; " he will never rest until all
the members of our moral suasion clubs become
Prohibitionists."

The meeting was closed soon afterwards.

" Mr. Rose is not one to sacrifice principle for

party," observed Mr. McFarlane. "When people ask what he is, in a political point of view, he tells them that he is 'a reformer of the reformers.'" "They inquire what he means by that ; and he tells them most candidly that he wants to make them all Teetotallers."

In coming down the stairs, Miss Wood remarked in a low tone, "Matilda, that is Mr. Rose just before us."

"Where ?"

"Over there, you blind beetle! He is putting his hand on the head of that little boy; Harry Hassard, I believe it is."

They came a few steps furthur down. "There, did you ever ?" exclaimed the spinster. "He is asking that lad near the foot of the stairs whether he has signed the Pledge ! It's just like Mr. Rose. I wonder if he in all his life missed an opportunity of inculcating Temperance !"

Ronald smiled. "I don't think so, Miss Wood. He is always seed-sowing. One night, in going to a Division-room, just within the city limits, he met a man with a pair of boots over his shoulder. Mr. Rose asked him whose house that was, pointing to a handsome one built by Davis, the brewer. The man knew to whom the property belonged, and Mr. Rose went on to remark that that fine house was built by those of us who drank beer. If money were spent on boots, or other necessaries, we had the worth of it; but what good did the beer do; money spent in that direction was thrown away. The man acknowledged the truth of Mr. Rose's words, and would no doubt think seriously over them."

"That was sowing the seed by the way-side," said Hattie, "and one day he will find it again."

" On another occasion," continued Ronald, " Mr. Rose, having been asked to speak at a Soiree in Grace Church, given by some friend to the members of a Coal and Fuel Association, who comprised several hundreds of poor people who had subscribed small sums of money weekly during the summer, and have it returned in the shape of coal and wood in the fall, took occasion to impress the importance of total abstinence upon them——"

" As usual," interrupted the spinster.

" And informed them that the money spent in

drinking and treating, if saved and put out at
interest, would buy them a house in the course
of ten years. It is needless to add that he
strongly advised them to let the liquor alone."

"I would say it was very admirable conduct
in anybody else," remarked Miss Wood; "but,
I don't like Mr. Rose."

"It is evident that he is always sowing the
good seed," said Hattie. "He never seems to forget it, morning, noon or night. There is not the
least doubt that God will bless his work; and it
rejoices me to think what an abundant harvest
he will have. 'They that be wise shall shine as
the brightness of the firmament; and they that
turn many to righteousness as the stars forever
and ever.'"

CHAPTER X.

UNITARIANISM.

"AUNT FANNY, are you coming to the concert of Crystal Fountain Division ? I cannot recommend it, for two of the best members will be away."

" Who are they ? "

" Mr. G. M. Rose and Mr. Daniel Rose."

"You only say that to induce me to come," peevishly remarked the spinster.

" If you don't believe it, perhaps you will glance at this article in the *Casket.*"

Miss Wood complied and then remarked, "This states that Mr. G. M. Rose and Mr. Daniel Rose are to speak at Napanee, on Tuesday, 26th November, during the session of the Grand Lodge of the Independent Order of Good Templars. What

a comfort," went on the spinster; " they cannot
possibly be in Toronto and Napanee at the same
time ; so of course I have no objection to go."

The Division-room was well filled ; it was decorated with numerous flags and some appropriate mottoes.   Miss Wood was congratulating
herself that the one member, who by his " fanatical views " would spoil the meeting for her, could
not possibly be present, when she heard Hattie
joyfully exclaim, " Oh, there's Mr. Rose ! "

The spinster turned furiously on her niece.
" You knew, you wicked creature," she snapped.

" I did not ; how could I possible know, Aunt
Fanny ? "

It turned out that untoward circumstances had
prevented Mr. Rose from getting to Napanee,
which was certainly a blessing for Crystal Fountain Division.

The meeting commenced.   An excellent programme had been provided.   Just before intermission, Mr. Rose was called upon for an address.
He went up on the platform and informed his
audience that one lady had requested him to
give a good long Temperance speech, while an-

other asked him to say only a few words; it was
impossible to satisfy both, therefore he would
please himself. The young men of our day professed to be afraid to marry on account of the
extravagance of the ladies; the real difficulty,
however, was in the liquor. He asked any
man to take pencil and paper, and reckon what five
drinks a day would amount to in a year. They
would find it would be a considerable sum. In
by-gone days, Brother Dilworth, Brother Rose
and others married for love; but now people
constantly thought of marrying for money, which
was a most preposterous idea. Mr. Rose has an
account called "sundries." He used to find that
his books did not balance; so he entered small
expenses that would otherwise have been forgotten, under the head of sundries, which in
a year, assumed almost alarming proportions.
The account was made up of items which were all
perfectly legitimate. The money spent by some on
liquor would easily support a little wife. Gooder-
ham & Worts, the distillers, had made their
money in five cent pieces. This Temperance
movement had saved a hundred thousand dollars

to the people of Toronto. Mr. Rose cordially invited all present, who did not belong to the Order
to unite themselves with it, playfully assuring
the ladies that it was frequently a method of getting husbands. Some people complained that
the Divisions were "sparking schools." He did
not object to the idea at all. Sparking was often
carried on in church; he had been guilty of it
himself when young. There could not be happier
marriages than those which originated in the Division-room. He could put his finger on half-a-dozen
couples, in that corner down there, who were making progress in that direction. An intermission
was always given for the very purpose of affording
the young people an opportunity of mutual acquaintance. "But" warmly continued Mr. Rose,
"the principal object of the Sons of Temperance, is
to do away with this confounded liquor traffic!"
He spoke of the evils it had caused, of the homes
and hearts it had made desolate; and emphatically urged that the thing that had caused "all
this devilment," should be totally put away. Mr.
Rose spoke of the privileges allowed the ladies
by the Order. They were on an equal footing

with the men, though it was not always so. For
a long time, strenuous opposition was made to
their becoming members ; but at last "young
blood" prevailed. He always wanted them
himself ; and could not understand why he
should be able to shew all possible affection
and esteem to ladies when outside, but not be
allowed to do so in the Division-room. He kindly
urged them to come and unite with us. Turning partly around he said in a low tone to the
chairman as though he were not quite sure, "Let
me see—do we make them ride that goat yet? Oh,
no, that belongs to the old way—" Then turning
again to the audience, he added, " Ladies, the only
goat you have to ride is to sign the Temperance
Pledge."—Some people would tell him that alcohol is a good creature of God. "God did not in-
vent alcohol," continued Mr. Rose, it is not found
in nature—*it is not a good creature of God, but
a creature of the devil.*" When it was first procured, by the process of distillation, it was not
used as a drink. It was then employed by the
ladies to beautify their complexions, but the men
use it now to paint their noses. The speaker

H

concluded by announcing an intermission for the
purposes before explained.

" I don't approve of it, at all !" said Miss Wood.

" Of sparking ? " inquired Hattie, with a laugh.

" No ; of Mr. Rose's strong language in regard
to the liquor traffic. In my opinion it was very
wrong ; but, doubtless, Ronald and yourself endorse those bad words in full."

Hattie nodded. " They were not bad! It is
impossible to speak too strongly of the accursed
thing," she said. " I am very glad that Mr. Rose
was present to give us some Temperance to-night ;
but I am really sorry for the people of Napanee ! "

A day or two afterwards, Miss Wood gravely
remarked to her niece, " I have just been think
ing of the various shades of religious thought
Between the Romanists on one hand, who believe
far too much, and the Unitarians on the other,
who scarcely believe anything, there are all grades
of opinion. The former are very superstitious ;
and, as for the latter, I have always regarded
them with positive horror. I would infinitely
prefer to be a Catholic than a Unitarian."

Mrs. Somerville was silent.

" My niece, if you have a grain of sense in that thick head of yours, answer me this—Do you think it possible for a Romanist to be saved ? "

" Oh, yes, Aunt Fanny. They love the Lord Jesus and trust in Him ; so, of course, they will be saved. Their faith is mixed up with superstition and error ; they have all that is necessary for salvation and a great deal more. I am speaking of true Catholics, who live up to what they profess. Aunt Fanny, do you remember reading about the young Italian monk ?"

" Was it a true case ?"

" Oh, yes ; perfectly true. On his death-bed he earnestly repeated the words of a noted father of his own Church. Unfortunately, I cannot remember the Latin, but the English of those words I shall never forget. He was stretched on his pallet, dying of consumption, when he exclaimed " *Good Jesu, Thy wounds are my merits—mine, mine, Lord Jesus!*" Then, with a farewell glance toward his friend, and a long, loving look on his crucifix, he died. That young monk was safely carried over Jordan in the arms of Jesus ; but, I believe the Unitarians prefer to swim ! "

" Then, they'll drown!" exclaimed the spinster.
" Not one Unitarian will ever enter heaven. They
will be lost—lost in sight of the shore and in
reach of the Life-boat, and it will serve them
right!"

There was no reply.

" What makes you look so pale, Hattie?"

Mrs. Somerville's lips trembled nervously as
she answered, " I hope when their feet touch the
cold waters of the Jordan, they will change their
minds, if not before, and allow Jesus to carry
them over. You know He is only waiting to do
it."

" Change their minds! Not a bit of it, my
niece. Do you not remember that old hymn you
used to sing which is set to music so slow, so
mournful, so dirge-like, that I verily believe you
English Church people stole it bodily from the
Romanists—

"As-the-tree-falls, so-must-it-lie ;
As-the-man-lives, so-will-he-die ;
As-the-man-dies, such-must-he-be
All through the days of Eternity."

Mrs. Somerville's voice faltered as she inquired,

" Aunt Fanny, do you mean that all Unitarians will go to hell ? "

" Whatever is the matter with you, my niece Is your father inclined that way ?"

Hattie shook her head.

" Ronald ?"

" Oh, no."

" Who then?" .

" It's no business of yours."

" You're an impertinent thing ! Of course Uni-tarians will be lost—every one of them. There may be some slight chance for Romanists; but, certainly none for them."

Mrs. Somerville raised her head and the colour came back to her cheeks. " I cannot agree with you, Aunt Fanny. Do you think that the author of ' Nearer, my God, to Thee,' is even now in the regions of the lost ? Oh no. The Rev Mr. Powis well said, the other Sunday, that we were far too narrow in condemning those who could not see as we did—the salvation of Christ was broader and deeper than we had any idea of—and it was very true. 'God is no respector of persons; but, in every nation, he that feareth Him, and worketh

righteousness, is accepted with Him.' I have no
doubt that there are numberless Unitarians who,
did they conscientiously believe that Jesus is our
atoning Saviour, would immediately embrace him.
Owing to some constitutional tendency, or other
causes, what seems so plain to us, is hidden from
them ; but, they love God and serve Him ; they
work for Christ, 'the Master,' in a way that puts
many of us orthodox Christians to shame. And
do you think that He will disown them at the
last ? I'll never believe it ! Christ will carry
them over Jordan, all unconscious of it, though
they may be——"

" Unconscious ! "

" Yes ;" and Hattie smiled. " Aunt Fanny, in
coming home late from an excursion last summer,
Mr. Rose's golden-haired baby was completely
tired out. It is only about two years old, and had
played around all the day. When the street-car
stopped at Clover Hill, it was fast asleep on its
sister's lap. Mr. Rose took it tenderly in his arms,
saying ' Poor little lassie.' The head of the baby
sank on its father's shoulder and he carried it out
of the car. It was perfectly safe in Mr. Rose's arms,

though all unconscious of it, and why should not Jesus carry them over Jordan, even though they be too fast asleep in His arms to know anything about it ; why should not His blood atone for them ? His righteousness be accounted theirs ? "

"That's nothing but supposition. I'll not hear a word more ; for it is useless to talk to such a person. There is neither reason nor religion in what you say. I have no doubt that Unitarians act quite conscientiously—love and serve God, according to the light they possess—but they will be lost for all that !" and Miss Wood walked out of the room.

"It is Aunt, who is unreasonable and not I," said Mrs. Somerville to herself. " The Lord Jesus knows right well that many, if not all, Unitarians would embrace Him as their Savour, could they only see that He made atonement for them. There is no doubt on my mind that all such will be saved, though a thousand Aunt Fannies should say the contrary ! "

CHAPTER XI.

"TRUE FREEDOM."

"MR. HASSARD in that chair ! It is really too bad," remarked Miss Wood.

" Don't you like him ? " innocently inquired Hattie.

" Yes, you stupid thing; don't you understand me; he will be morally sure to call upon Mr. Rose ! "

" Oh, I hope he will ! "

The spinster scowled upon her niece as she replied, " Mr. Rose spoke at the special concert last Saturday ; at Crystal Fountain Division last Tuesday ; and, as Hassard is in that chair, we shall probably be favoured with another dose of Prohibition to-night."

"I'm sure I don't know what we should do without Mr. Rose," replied Mrs. Somerville earnestly ; "there is not one in the Club who is thankful enough to God for him."

· After various songs had been given to the audience, the chairman arose and stated that we came here for an object, viz., to get signatures to the Pledge, as well as new recruits to help us in our work. He said that when the Club was first started, we used to have several Temperance talks every evening ; and now, he would call upon one who had for *a short time* been working for the cause—say between thirty and forty years ; one who had always been foremost in this and every other total abstinence society, viz., Brother Rose, and he hoped he would put his best foot foremost to-night.

Mr. G. M. Rose stepped on the platform and playfully remarked that he was ashamed of his "best foot," for he had got it in the mud ; however, he assured us that his shoes were clean and bright when he left home. If a man, more especially a Scotchman, came to him seeking work or assistance, he always looked first at his boots. If he were slovenly about his feet, it invariably happened that he was a drinking character. The lower animals would not use intoxicating liquor; take one of the most despised among them, a pig for instance—who ever heard of a pig getting drunk? "You may say that he wallows in the mire—he does it to clean himself." After expressing his pleasure that the chairman had spoken as he had done, Mr. Rose said he would go further still and declared that we ought to have a Temperance talk of three minutes or so between every song. Many young men thought it a manly thing to drink; it was, on the contray, a mean thing. He told them of various places, such as the reading-room of the Young Men's Christian Association, etc., where they could spend an hour or two of an evening with far more pleasure and profit than they could obtain in a saloon. He then defied them to assert that anything good could ever be learned in a bar-room. "Some young men have to be taken by the shoulders and *made to do right.*" People complained that we wanted to deprive them of their liberty; it was not so, we wished to give them true freedom—freedom from their evil appetites and passions. If a man wanted unrestricted liberty he must go into a foreign country among savages. Our legal enactments were for the restraining of evil, and if we went a step further and passed a prohibitory law for the whole Dominion, we should be advancing in the direction of universal freedom.

"Now, are you satisfied, Hattie?" growled the old maid, when she once more reached her home.

"No, I'm not, Mr. Rose never yet spoke long enough to satisfy me. Aunt Fanny, a letter came from Prince Edward Island to-day. Perhaps you would like to read it."

"Yes; how are Theodore and Isabel?"

"All right—the letter is from their little girl."

"Janie; give it to me, my niece; I want to see if that lass is improving."

Mrs. Somerville handed it over, merely remarking that Janie wrote very neatly.

Miss Wood perused the letter in silence, until near the end, when a wrathful expression came to her lips, and she exclaimed, "Just listen to what the young one says: 'I can play all the pieces you

marked for me in those Temperance books ; and
some that are not marked.   I can play " Prohibition " real nice.'   Wouldn't I ' Prohibition ' that
lass, if only I had hold of her.   Yes, it is just like
you to laugh, Hattie ; there's some of your work."

" Oh, don't give me the credit of it.   Isabel has
good, sound common sense, and has educated her
daughter properly.   Janie will no doubt prove a
blessing to her Dunkinite parents."

" Did Theodore vote for the Dunkin Act before
he left North York ? "

" Of course he did, Aunt Fanny."

The spinster frowned, but made no reply.

" Ronald and I are going to the Executive meet-
g of the Central Club next Monday night, to
ee how they manage the business part of these as-
sociations."

" Will they admit visitors ? "

" They do now—all who are members of the
Club."

When Monday evening arrived they went according to agreement. Mrs. Somerville coaxed her
aunt to go, assuring her that Mr. Rose was not
in the habit of attending the executive meetings

for he could not spare the time, so she need not be afraid of seeing him. Miss Wood felt very doubtful at first, but finally consented. The members came in twos and threes; soon the spinster whispered angrily to Ronald, " You have both deceived me again—that's Mr. Rose !" It was near the close of the term, and that gentleman had found it almost necessary to be present on several occasions, but the Professor and his bride-elect were not aware of the fact.

During the evening, Mr. Rose strongly advocated having more Temperance in the Saturday-night meetings and declared that he would not come down all through the winter merely to listen to a five-cent concert. He came to do good. We ought not to be satisfied without fruit. The audience seemed to have lost all sympathy with the members of the Club ; and it would get worse and worse, until they would not listen to a Temperance speech at all. At our last special concert he had invited a friend to come, who afterwards frankly informed Mr. Rose that he would not have known it was a Temperance meeting at all, except for the address given by him. Mr. Rose

said he felt complimented by the remark; but
things ought not to be in such a condition. He
advocated short speeches by the reformed men.

Mr. Hassard declared that they had often been
invited to speak, but always declined.

"They would not refuse if *I* asked them,"
firmly replied Mr. Rose; and further stated, "that,
if he were in the chair, things would be differently arranged."

"What a pity that he did not accept the position of President," remarked Mrs. Somerville on
the way home.

"My dear, it is a great deal of work to put
upon one who has already so much on his hands,"
answered Mr. McFarlane. "Do you want his
health to break down? Mr. Rose is not made of
iron, remember."

"I know it," sadly replied Hattie; "and I wish
he would take better care of himself."

The spinster listened to their conversation in
silence, and would not open her mouth all the way
home.

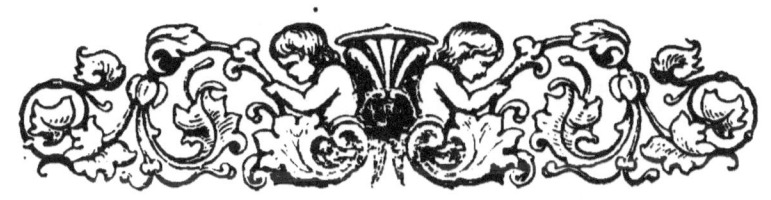

CHAPTER XII.

THE GRAND DIVISION.

"GOOD-BYE, Aunt Fanny."

"Good riddance!" jubilantly returned the spinster, as she retreated into her study. "Now, I'll take advantage of her absence and write, for the time will go all too quickly."

Which it did; for in a few days Mrs. Somerville returned from the annual Session of the Grand Division, which had just been held in Galt. No sooner had she set her foot in Miss Wood's domains, than the spinster eagerly inquired, "Well, what kind of a time did you have—what of those mass-meetings from which you expected so much?"

" They disappointed me, Aunt Fanny; I did
not go to the first at all."

" Why not ?"

" The speakers were advertised, and Mr. G. M.
Rose positively refused to allow his name to be
placed on the list. I took it so entirely for
granted that he would give us a long address, that
I was too bitterly disappointed to go out the first
evening at all."

Miss Wood laughed. " Well, you liked the
meetings of the Grand Division proper. Doubtless, Mr. Rose joined in the discussions. Now, do
go on and tell me that there was not a single representative who was fit to · hold a candle to
him !"

" Aunt Fanny, had you been there, you would
have seen how exactly you have spoken the
truth !" replied Mrs. Somerville earnestly. " There
was not a representative present who could in
any respect compare with Brother Rose. I always knew that he was as noble as he looks; and,
never did he appear more so than in that Grand
Division. Aunt Fanny, I was so proud of him !"

" Oh, I dare say. Were you actually foolish

enough to imagine that all the representatives would be Mr. Roses? Ah, I knew you would be sadly disappointed. Give me an account of the session."

"The address, or rather report, of Mr. Millar, the retiring Grand Worthy Patriarch, interested me much. Among other points, he spoke of Lectures Cadets and Bands of Hope, Church-work, Sabbath-School-work, Prohibition, including the Dunkin and Scott Acts, Newspaper for the Order, Reform Clubs, etc., and, towards the close, he says, "To George Maclean Rose, Past Grand Worthy Patriarch, I have been, on more than one occasion, deeply indebted for his readiness in assuming duties away from home, at a time when I was unable to leave; and I take the present opportunity of publicly thanking him."

"Is that all you are going to read of the report?" asked the spinster, impatiently.

"I hope to give you the benefit of it in full, when you have time to listen; but this part, I thought very beautiful, and it touched my heart, Aunt Fanny."

"By all means let me hear it!"

I

Hattie read, "I have heard it said that we are too slow for this age of progress. I don't think we are. I look around this Council Chamber and I see men who, with thirty-five years' experience, bring to bear upon our deliberations the wisdom which such service has given them. I see men in the prime of life, with here and there a 'silver thread among the golden,' who for a quarter of a century have gone weekly to the Division."

"Yes, I know why it affected you—Mr. G. M. Rose has 'silver threads' among his golden-red hair; and, for twenty-five years, or more, he has faithfully attended the meetings of the Sons of Temperance. Mr. Millar expressed it very nicely, Hattie; I don't deny that."

"Aunt Fanny, Matilda wanted me to coax father to dye his hair, which, you know, is getting very white. I felt so annoyed that I could have boxed her ears. Gray hairs don't spoil anyone. The Bible says they are 'a crown of glory.'"

The spinster's black locks had changed of late to iron-gray; and she immediately replied, "That is the most sensible remark I have heard you make for a long while, my niece. Your father would be a perfect fright if he used any odious dye-stuff; and, Hattie," she added mischievously, " do you think that those 'silver threads among the golden' do in the slightest degree spoil Mr. Rose ?"

"No, Aunt Fanny, I should think not," emphatically returned Mrs. Somerville. "You would spoil him though with a vengeance if you made them anything else !"

"You have a little sense, after all, my niece ; and I can actually agree with you for once."

" A marvellous thing, truly ; for we differ on almost every conceivable point."

" Now you may tell me about the business part of the session."

" How can I ? You are not a member of the Order."

" Nonsense ; just give me general information. A good deal was published in the daily newspapers."

" Those reports were written by Mr. Rose."

" Were they ? I wish I had known that in time and I would not have read them. Go on, I say—"

" The report of the Committee on the Address was taken up clause by clause and interested me very much. Unfortunately there was such an echo in the Hall, that I failed in hearing several of the speeches, especially one by Mr. Rose. He was standing at some distance from where I sat, and it was impossible to distinguish it all."

" I'll warrant it was on Prohibition !"

" Yes, *it was on Prohibition* Mr. Rose stated that he had never cast a vote for a man who was not pledged to support Temperance measures. Again and again his voice was fairly drowned in thunders of applause."

" All things considered, there was no wonder you could not hear him."

" The next representative who spoke thought ' that Brother Rose ought to go further than that and only vote for total abstainers.' Mr. Rose was immediately on his feet again, emphatically declaring 'that he never cast a vote, save for a Teetotaller !' Several of the representatives mentioned the Dunkin Bill. Aunt Fanny, it is a good law when enforced, and that can be done, for so it was stated positively."

"Is that all you are going to tell me?"

Mrs. Somèrville smiled. "There was a long, tiresome discussion about credentials, as to who were rightful representatives and who were not. The Report of the Committee on the Address will be published with the minutes, etc. I hope to read it to you as soon as it comes from the press. There was the initiation of members into the Grand Division, which was quite an impressive ceremony ; also, the election and installation of officers for the ensuing year. There were a few unpleasant items of business to settle, which took up the time in a somewhat tedious way. One was a dispute in a subordinate Division about the location of a Temperance Hall. Much bitter feeling had been displayed by the members of the said Division, neither side being at all inclined to give in. Both parties were confident they were in the right, and considerable ill feeling followed as a matter of course."

" Yes, and, doubtless Mr. Rose, so hot-tempered as he is, would only make the affair worse."

" That's all you know about it, Aunt Fanny ! He did more than anyone else to settle the diffi-

culty in a quiet, peaceable way ; and, in a manner, as far as possible, satisfactory to both.   He
poured oil on the troubled waters; and things are
likely to go all right in that locality now.   There
will probably be two active Divisions instead of
one—rivals, it may be, but generous ones—and
for that you have to thank Mr. Rose."

"Well, go on, " said the spinster glumly, who
was determined not to acknowledge herself mistaken.

" There was considerable difference of opinion
in regard to business matters.   Several of the
representatives were factious and quarrelsome.
There are such persons in every organization, and
some of the meetings were very stormy."

The eyes of the old maid sparkled maliciously.
" Hattie, will you answer me a question ?—It is
nothing about the business at all."

"Oh, certainly, if I can."

" You say there was warmth of feeling mani-
fested on several occasions—how often did Mr.
Rose lose his temper ? "

"Not once ! " indignantly returned Hattie.

"Do you mean to tell me, that, during all the

heated discussions of a stormy session, he never got angry ?"

" Oh, he was angry, sometimes ; and fully as hot as he usually is !"

"I thought so!" triumphantly exclaimed the spinster." It is a great satisfaction to me that anything happened to vex him. You look as though you were going to eat me, my niece."

"Never fear; you are far too sour for that !"

" You are a deceitful thing, as I've often told you. Why did you say that Mr. Rose did not lose his temper ?"

" Because it was the truth. He was hot and angry enough, of course ; so much so, that Mr. Millar afterwards remarked, that if Mr. Rose and his opponent could only have had their photographs taken, while they both stood on the floor at once, gazing at each other, what a nice picture they would have made !"

The old maid laughed. " How I wish I had seen them ! But you eat your own words, Hattie. What you do understand by loss of temper, anyway ?"

" Why, Aunt Fanny, getting so angry as to

lose control of oneself, and saying and doing things in a fit of passion that one would be sorry for an hour afterwards. That is an altogether different thing. St. Paul tells us 'to be angry and sin not.' Christ himself was angry with those provoking Scribes and Pharisees; but I am sure He did not lose His temper!"

"You aggravate me beyond measure, Hattie! How often do I tell you not to drag the Bible into our unseemly disputes! You would fain make me believe that Mr. Rose is an angel; but I assure you he wants considerably more than the wings to make him one!"

Mrs. Somerville laughed.

"Oh, I knew you would not agree with me!" said Miss Wood. Then looking sharply at her niece, she added, "You are tired with travelling, Hattie. I will not ask you anything further until after dinner, when you shall read aloud the Report of the Grand Worthy Patriarch."

"Very well, Aunt Fanny."

CHAPTER XIII.

"PROHIBITION HAS COME!"

"NOW, I am ready for that report."

"What a quantity of fancy-work you have there, Aunt Fanny!"

"Yes; another Church-bazaar," impatiently returned Miss Wood. "I would far rather be in my study. Now, take that pamphlet and commence."

Mrs. Somerville obeyed, and read the reports of the Grand Worthy Patriarch, Grand Scribe and Grand Treasurer. Then, laying down the pamphlet, she remarked, "In one of the discussions, Mr. Rose spoke of those people who separate Temperance from religion. He held, on the contrary, that Temperance is a part of religion."

" I'm sure it is a part of his, at all events ! And so a number of the representatives put up at the ' Queen's ?'"

" Yes, and a happy party they were. I hope they demonstrated to the satisfaction of the hotel-keeper, that it was possible to be merry ' without the aid of wine.'"

" So you got along all right and enjoyed yourself? It was a pity that Ronald could not go too. You had very gloomy weather nearly all the time."

" Yes, and on our way to the Town Hall, we had to cross a bridge over the Grand River. A new one was in process of erection, and the only way was to walk on some slippery planks. It was certainly a dangerous place."

" Was there not a railing or other protection?"

" No, indeed, Aunt Fanny. If your foot slipped there was nothing to prevent your going over and being drowned. I did not mind crossing it alone in the day-time, but thought it scarcely right to do so in the dark ; for there were no lights or anything of that kind, and the river was swollen with the recent rains."

" What culpable negligence on the part of the authorities. Were you afraid, Hattie ? "

" On my own account ? Oh, no."

" On whose then ? "

" Why, I was afraid of Mr. Rose ; and would infinitely have preferred that every one of us had gone over and been drowned in preference to him."

" Yourself included? "

" Of course ; I am not worth anything to the cause. And all the Grand Division put together are not equal to him."

" So far as Temperance is concerned, you mean. That is just your own private opinion. I do wish that Grand Division could hear you ; how highly complimented they would feel."

" Much they would care, Aunt Fanny."

" I think, my niece, that you are not a disciple of Professor Tyndall, but believe in prayer. Doubtless you did not fail to ask that that exceedingly precious Mr. Rose should be under the special guardianship of our Saviour, and that He would not suffer him to get drowned."

Hattie smiled.

" Did you forget, my niece ? "

" What ? To pray for Mr. Rose ? I never forget. He is too closely connected with the Temperance cause for that."

" Just as I thought. Now tell me about those mass-meetings. Did you go to the second ? "

"Yes, and heard an address from Mr. G. W. Ross, our Prohibition leader in Parliament. I took a good look at him, Aunt Fanny, as he stood on the floor of the Division room. Mr. Ross is very like the photograph of him which I procured from the 'Topley Studio' at Ottawa. All the parliamentary notables may be gotten from the same place, and many other public men as well. Mr. W. J. Topley is evidently a business man and remarkably courteous and prompt in filling any order that may be sent. I have had several photographs of Temperance men from his studio, and they have all given good satisfaction. You did not see the last one I got, Aunt Fanny. It is a 10 x 8 picture of Mr. G. M. Rose."

" No, but you shall just show it to me now, so you shall."

Mrs. Somerville left the room and soon returned with the photograph in her hand.

"It is beautifully taken," remarked the spinster. "Now laugh, Hattie, do. Mind you I did not say there was anything beautiful about the original. Mr. Rose looks as though he were pondering some matter of weighty importance. Prohibition probably," she added, with a sneer.

Mrs. Somerville carried the treasured picture safely away, and then returned to her aunt.

"Go on about the mass-meeting, my niece. Did you like Mr. Ross ?"

"Of course, that is nothing new. It is rare indeed that I do not like a Temperance speaker, whoever he may be. The Rev. Mr. Porter also gave a short address, and urged us all to take Christ for our foundation, and then to build upon Him as grand and noble a character as we pleased. Mr. J. W. Manning spoke at some length. His remarks were very good. Towards the close he mentioned the plague-stricken cities of the South, described the ravages of yellow fever, and how anxiously the people waited for the only remedy—the frost. At length, after great suffering and many deaths, they awoke one morning to find the ground white ; and immediately the glad cry was heard, 'The frost has come ! The frost has come !' Mr. Manning then went on to describe the miseries caused by intemperance, and the remedy therefor. The day was at hand when the joyful shout should ring from the Atlantic to the Pacific—from Gaspé to British Columbia—' Prohibition has come ! Prohibition has come ! ' "

The spinster frowned. " You may save yourself the trouble of telling me anything further about the mass-meeting," she said coldly.

A sudden thought struck Mrs. Somerville, and she inquired, " Aunt Fanny, have you seen those ' mental ' photograph albums ? "

" You mean those that require you to answer, in writing, a whole page of questions, such as your favourite colour, flower, minister, etc., and not content with that, would fain make you acknowledge, in that most unpleasantly public manner, your peculiar faults and failings. Yes, I've seen them, Hattie ; and nothing should ever induce me to fill up one of those pages, unless indeed I might leave three or four blanks ' "

" The first I saw was at Galt, Aunt Fanny ;

and one of the pages bore the name of Mr .G. M.
Rose."

" What were the answers, Hattie ? " eagerly
inquired Miss Wood.

" I cannot remember all, but will tell you a part.
Mr. Rose's favourite colour is lilac ; his favourite
flower, pansy ; his favourite object in nature, a
sound mind in a well-developed body ; his favourite character in history, Jesus Christ. The things
he disliked were ignorance and vulgarity ; the
sweetest words, in his opinion, were, ' my darling.'
His idea of pleasure was, apart from business,
reading and attending Temperance meetings ;
his motto—' Dare to do right !' "

" Hattie, is that all you remember ? Those
questions that related to personal faults and
failings, I'll warrant, were left blank !"

" Oh no, Aunt Fanny. Mr. Rose answered
them all in the most straight-forward manner."

" Indeed, that is more than I expected. It is
useless to ask you to tell me : I see that very
plainly. Well, I hope you are convinced, by
reading it in his own hand-writing, that Mr. Rose
has some slight failing of one kind or other."

Mrs. Somerville answered calmly," I thought
every man who ever lived had that, Aunt Fanny,
with the single exception of our Lord Jesus
Christ.   Miss Wood was silent for some time.
" Hattie," she remarked, at length, " Ronald will
be home to-morrow, . It was lonesome without
either of you.   I hope you will settle in Toronto
after your marriage."

" Pray don't speak of that yet ; there is time
enough.   How long are you going to work for
that bazaar ? "

" At least three months, now and again.   You
must make up your mind to play, sing, read, and
otherwise amuse me, while I am at work."

" All right.   Just leave those dolls for me.   I
will dress them and tic blue sashes over their left
shoulders, to imitate ' Band of Hope ' girls."

The spinster gladly pushed the dolls over to her
niece, who. took them up to her room.   An hour
passed.   Miss Wood wondered what was the
reason Hattie did not come down, and went upstairs to seek her.   She was half-asleep, with
" Greg's Creed of Christendom " in her hand.
The old maid snatched the volume and threw it

into the fire. To her surprise, Hattie made no attempt to rescue it from the flames.

"My dear niece, you, of all others, really ought not to read such books !" said Miss Wood, in an anxious tone.

" Why should it injure me, more than the generality of people ? "

"Because, Hattie, for you there is no middle ground. If you were not a Christian, you would be an out-and-out infidel."

" I know that as well as you can tell me, Aunt Fanny."

" My poor, unfortunate niece, " groaned the spinster, " you are at the mercy of the first sceptic who may cross your path."

Mrs. Somerville saw that her relative was in genuine distress, and hastened to relieve her mind. " Aunt Fanny, a religion that will do to die by, will also do to live by—won't it ? "

" Yes, indeed."

" Were you ever very ill—so ill that you could, tell by the words and looks of those around your bed that they did not think it possible for you to recover ? "

J

The old maid shivered. "No," she said, "I never was, and have hardly had a week's illness in my life. The thought of death is extremely unpleasant."

"Oh, Aunt Fanny, it is not bad when you come to it. No Christian has any reason to be afraid to die."

"I have often wished to ask you about it, my niece, but feared to do so, thinking the subject as unwelcome to you as it is to me. You were so ill as to be reported dead. I believe you expected to get better yourself—dying people often do that—but did it not occur to you that those around might be right and you wrong?"

"Oh yes, Aunt Fanny, I felt how easily I might be mistaken; and in that case a few hours would have ended everything. That was as clear as daylight, and I thought of the last messages I would send home."

"Hattie, it makes me shiver to think of it. You were far from all your friends out there in the bush. It was one of the most severe winters I ever remember to have seen, and you were lying in a miserable little room in a log hut, the wind blowing through the cracks, with both minister and doctor miles aways. A worse place to die in, could not well have been found."

" 'The thought of a minister never entered my head. I wanted the doctor though to relieve me if possible of that agonizing pain."

" Did you cry ? "

" Oh no ; I assure you, Aunt Fanny, when you come to that you will be past crying. One of my trustees fetched the doctor through the snow-blocked roads on that bitter morning, and glad I was to see him. That day was one of such intense physical agony that I never attempted to say my prayers, a thing which has not happened either before or since."

" Hattie, did you not pray at all ? "

" Oh yes, but not in a connected way, as we always do. The doctor and the wives of my trustees were close around my bed, but Jesus was closer still, and His presence glorified that desolate little room. Do you suppose I did not speak to Him ? Yes, indeed ; and I felt how happily I could die with His arms around me ! Not having been there a week, the people were entire strangers,

and not one of my loved ones could have got
to me in time; but the Lord Jesus was more
than sufficient, and right well I knew that he
would not let me die alone. Aunt Fanny, all the
Mr. Gregs in Christendom could not blot out the
remembrance of that hour. If Jesus were not
God as well as man, how could He have comforted
and sustained me then? How could He have
been present in that lonely hut in North Hastings? Aunt Fanny, I used to think of death
quite nervously before; but since that time all
has been so different. When I come to die, no
swimming over Jordan for me; I will let Jesus
carry me over in His arms and thank Him for
it."

Miss Wood looked inexpressibly relieved. " Oh,
Hattie, why did you not tell me that before ? "

" Because I was not brought up a Methodist,
and as a natural consequence generally keep such
things to myself. I should not have told you
now, but you were so anxious about me. Why
do you suppose I read Mr. Greg's book ? Not
from curiosity alone; but you see people might
put those and similiar objections to us, which it

would be difficult to answer on the spur of the
moment. We ought to be able to give a reason
for the hope that is in us."

"Just so, my dear. And I trust you will
study Paley's 'Evidences,' as a means to that desirable end," said the spinster as she left the
room.

CHAPTER XIV.

A MODEL CHAIRMAN.

"WORSE and worse—Mr. Rose in that chair!" exclaimed Miss Wood.

"I'm very glad," said the Professor; " no doubt we shall have an excellent meeting."

"It was only yesterday that he returned from the Grand Division," remarked Hattie, " to the proceedings of which he paid close attention, as well as taking upon himself the task of preparing reports for the papers. I am afraid he must be tired out. He was, at all events, at the close of the session; and an accumulation of business matters in Toronto would not allow of any time for rest since then."

"Aren't you glad to see him act as president, *pro tem.*?" asked Miss Wood,

"Yes, indeed, Aunt Fanny. I only hope that he won't undertake too much and wear himself out."

The meeting commenced. Mr. Rose read the hymn beginning, "All hail the power of Jesus' name," which was then sung by the choir. Instead of sitting down by the table and merely rising (as the other occupants of that chair had been in the habit of doing, more especially of late), he often came to the very front of the platform and did so at the opening address.

"I would defy anybody to make an automaton of Mr. Rose," whispered the spinster; "he is far too much in earnest for that."

The chairman stated that we came here for an object, to elevate one another to a higher level, to spend an evening sociably together, and more particularly to induce all to become total abstainers. When we had persuaded men to sign the pledge, we found that was not enough; it was necessary to put our arms around them, as it were, to give them a substitute for the amusements of the saloon and bar-room. So we held a social meeting for that purpose on Saturday

night. However, we were going to have a little
variation this evening ; we would have some
temperance speeches. A very nice programme
had been put into his hands and the audience
must be in sympathy with us and take part. " I
have got you all down on the programme," continued Mr. Rose, " you are going to join in singing
hymns, when I ask you to do so; and you are
going to obey me, as those on the platform will
do—" and he glanced at the choir and speakers.
He then called on a young lady for a piano solo,
which was followed by a song from another lady.
Mr. Rose then came forward and told how encouraged he had been, during the last week, by
the progress of temperance in the West. On the
Tuesday previous, he had been away at Galt,
where delegates from all parts of the Province
were assembled. There were over one hundred
of them, and he personally only knew about half a
dozen; but they were all as one, and discussed
temperance matters for two days. He said he
enjoyed it very much and had a glorious time !
In the evenings, they held mass-meetings ; on the
first, the hall which would hold six or seven

hundred people, was filled; but, on the second night, it was not large enough to accommodate the audience. Mr. Rose graphically related the story of the workingman who, when asked how he became a convert to teetotalism, would invariably answer, " The little shoes, they did it all !" He then called on Brother Moore for a few words, inquiring whether it was the loving embraces of a wife or some other cause that made him become a teetotaller.

Mr. Moore came forward and acknowledged that he had been drinking for thirty or forty years ; and, for a part of that time, very heavily. A man, who had thus been saturated with liquor, could not get it out of his system all at once. He signed the pledge eighteen months ago and kept it ever since. It took him a year to get sober ; for, during that time, his brain got clearer and he felt better in every way ; and, for the last six months, he had been a man again. The audience warmly applauded him as he returned to his seat.

Mr. Rose then came to the front of the platform and told them that after that speech we

would have our old battle song. If he had
a weakness for any hymn in the book, it was the
first—" Hold the Fort." He then proceeded to
read the hymn, or a portion of it, which was sung
both by the choir and audience with zest.

An amusing duet followed, and then some
"anvil music," as Mr. Rose very characteristically
named it, consisting of instrumental solos on
small blocks of wood, by Professor Curtis.

Mr. Rose then called on Bro. Black for a short
temperance talk, who at once complied, though
he owned he would rather not. His words had
a good effect. He said that signing the pledge had
made him a better man in his home, which senti-
ment, it was very evident, favourably impressed
the audience.

Mr. Rose said that if we had done nothing else
but save those two men, we had had our reward.
Instead of that, there were hundreds and thousands whom under God we had been the means
of raising up and making their homes happy.
It was said by the other side that the delegates
to the Grand Division carried their brandy-flasks
in their pockets; " but, if we did," said Mr. Rose,

"we managed to keep them there, which was more than they could do!"

("Does he mean that they carried liquor with them," inquired Miss Wood, in astonishment. Hattie could not help laughing. "Surely you know, Aunt Fanny, that Mr. Rose is only in play.")

The chairman then announced an intermission of five minutes and hoped that the brothers and sisters would go around in the audience and persuade the people to come forward and sign. The choir sang, "Only an armour-bearer." Mr. Rose called out to the boys to come and sign the Pledge; and himself set the example of going among the audience, for he came down from the platform and went all around the hall, and not in vain.

Then a Temperance reading was given, followed by a recitation entitled "The Orange and the Green," which was of such an amicable nature that it could not fail to please both the partisans of the lily and the shamrock. "I like both the Orange and the Green," said Mr. Rose, "they are pretty colours, but I don't like those party fights." Then he said that it was time to bring the meeting

to a close.   There were some young men near the
door whom he wished to get.   His eloquence had
been lost upon two of them, but he was glad to
say that three or four had come forward and
signed the Pledge.   He called on Mr. McFederis
for the appeal, which was immediately made, and
then Mr. Rose gave out the hymn, "Work, for the
night is coming," which was sung by the choir
and audience, and afterwards the meeting was
closed.

"What a marvellous difference from the enter-
tainments we have had so long," said Hattie,
"Did you ever see such a chairman ? " she triumphantly added.

"No," growled the spinster, "one Mr. G.M.Rose
is quite sufficient. Do you suppose I want a dozen
like him ? No, indeed ! "

When they reached home, Miss Wood inquired,
"My niece, did you ever see Mr. Rose act as chairman before ? "

"Not of the meeting of a Reform Club, but I
am told that Temperance societies frequently pre-
vail upon him to act in that capacity. About a
year ago, or more, there was a complimentary sup-

per tendered by the Women's Christian Temperance Union to their retiring President. It was a
pleasant little social party. The ladies brought
their husbands with them, and at about nine
o'clock, Mr. Rose was asked to take the chair, and
some speeches were made. In his opening address,
he spoke of the folly of shutting out the men
from the Women's Temperance Convention which
had just been held. It was an entirely useless
proceeding, for the wives would tell their husbands all about the matter as soon as they
got home, as his wife had told him. He spoke,
too, of the degraded condition of women, in the
olden time and eastern countries. Mr. Rose said
that it was our Saviour Jesus Christ who took
woman by the hand and raised her to her true
position in society."

"A sensible remark," muttered the spinster.
"Hattie," she suddenly inquired, "how did you
pass Thanksgiving Day at Galt?"

"In attending the morning and afternoon sessions of the Grand Division and the Temperance
mass-meeting at night. It was very different
from last Thanksgiving Day—you remember we

went to the ' breakfast for the poor,' given by
the Women's Christian Temperance Union and
Central Club.   There were a number of boys
present who were more or less ragged and
dirty."

"Yes; and how, when breakfast was over,
this, that and the other man spoke not at all to
your satisfaction, for they told the boys not to
steal, not to lie, not to swear; but the idea of
drink never seemed to enter their old fogy heads.
I saw, Hattie, how your look of uneasiness turned
to one of anger, as the children began to go
out; and I noticed, too, how your face brightened
when Mr. Rose came forward to speak.
There was no danger of further disappointment;
you were sure of some temperance then!"

"Yes, indeed, Aunt Fanny.   That meeting
would have been a perfect failure, had Brother
Rose not been there.   Do you remember how he
spoke of the time when he was a lad, the same
as those before him; and added, as he pointed
to one of the group, " like that little red-headed
boy down there, only my face was clean."
That child would no doubt think on what

he had heard and wash himself before he went to the next Temperance meeting. Mr. Rose spoke to such good purpose that I do not remember one of the little urchins going away without signing the pledge and having a blue ribbon pinned on his coat."

" Oh, yes ; I remember all about it," was the somewhat peevish reply.

When the spinster went upstairs, in about half-an-hour's time, she saw a light burning in the room of her niece. Putting her head in at the door, she inquired, " What are you doing, Hattie ? It is time to go to bed."

" I am writing for father, while it is fresh in my memory, an account of that model temperance meeting."

" Of that model chairman, you mean," snapped the old maid, as she closed the door with a bang.

CHAPTER XV.

FAVOURITE HYMNS.

" AUNT Fanny, are you sick ? " asked Mrs. Somerville anxiously. " You did not get out to church, or to the experience meeting either."

" I don't feel well. What was it like—were there many present ? "

" There were such a large number of young men ; far more than usual. I know what brought them ; it was Mr. Rose's admirable method of conducting the meeting last night."

" I don't believe it ; and my opinion is as good as yours, any day."

" Then why did they come, Aunt Fanny ? "

"Oh, I don't know; perhaps Mr. Stark had exerted a greater influence than usual."

"Nothing of the kind. The meetings have slowly increased in both numbers and interest; but never since last winter did such crowds of young men come in. Why they must have filled one-fourth of the hall!"

"And Mr. Rose, our 'admirable' chairman last night, brought them there!"

"I firmly believe that he did!"

"Nothing would ever convince you—have it your own way, you contrary thing!"

There was silence for some time. At length Miss Wood asked her niece to play and sing for her. "None of those lively pieces, remember, that go rattling through one's brain : give me something of a quiet, soothing nature."

"I will, Aunt Fanny," said Mrs. Somerville; "have you any choice?"

"Yes; play 'Rock of Ages,' and 'Jesus, Lover of my soul.' After them, some of your own favourites. Those two hymns are dear to the hearts of Christians the world over."

Hattie complied, and then asked, "Will you

K

have ' Paradise,' Aunt Fanny ?   I am very fond
of it."

" Yes, and so am I."

Mrs. Somerville sang :—

> " O Paradise, O Paradise,
>> Who doth not crave for rest ?
>> Who would not seek the happy land
>> Where they that loved are blest ?
>>> Where loyal hearts and true
>>> Stand ever in the light,
>>> All rapture through and through,
>>> In God's most holy sight.

> " O Paradise, O Paradise,
>> I want to sin no more,
>> I want to be as pure on earth
>> As on thy spotless shore ;
>>> Where loyal hearts and true
>>> Stand ever in the light,
>>> All rapture through and through,
>>> In God's most holy sight.

> '' Lord Jesu, King of Paradise,
>> O keep me in Thy love,
>> And guide me to that happy land
>> Of perfect rest above ;
>>> Where loyal hearts and true
>>> Stand ever in the light,
>>> All rapture through and through
>>> In God's most holy sight."

"That is very sweet, Hattie; sing something else."   •

" Will you have ' Angels of Jesus ?' "

" Oh, no; it seems Romish to me."

Mrs. Somerville smiled, and her aunt impatiently added, " You have such a number of favourite hymns, my niece, that it is probably hard to know which to choose. Sing the verse you like the best of that ' Angels of Jesus.' "

Hattie immediately obeyed.

" Rest comes at length, though life be long and dreary,
    The day must dawn, and darksome night be past ;
Faith's journey ends in welcome to the weary,
    And Heaven, the heart's true home, will come at last.
Angels of Jesus, Angels of Light,
Singing to welcome the pilgrims of the night."

" Now, do give me something composed by a Romanist," sarcastically remarked Miss Wood.

" Oh, certainly ; will you have ' Dies iræ, Dies illa ?' you know that, though it was composed by a monk there is nothing in it that a Protestant can object to. It is the grandest hymn on the 'Last judgment' that was ever written."

" Very well, go on."

" Day of wrath ! O day of mourning ;
See fulfilled the prophet's warning ;
Heaven and earth in ashes burning !
Oh, what fear man's bosom rendeth,
-When from Heaven the Judge desendeth
On whose sentence all dependeth ! " etc.

Hattie sang the long hymn and then asked if her aunt were not tired.

" No.   Is not that a fearful description ?   It makes one shudder to think what the reality will be!"

" Now, I'll sing you a hymn by John Wesley :

' Jesus, Thy blood and righteousness
My beauty are, my glorious dress ;
'Midst flaming worlds, in these arrayed
With joy shall I lift up my head.

' Bold shall I stand in Thy great day ;
For who aught to my charge shall lay ?
Fully absolved through these I am,
From sin and fear, from guilt and shame.'

' I am not a Methodist," said Hattie, but must confess (with all due deference to that worthy monk) that I like Wesley's hymn better than Dies iræ, Dies illa ! "

"So do I," said the old maid. "Now, Hattie, go as far as possible in the other direction, give us a Unitarian hymn, do."

"Certainly," and Mrs. Somerville sang "Nearer, my God, to Thee."

"Oh, that is orthodox enough, otherwise, I am sure, you would not sing it."

"No, Aunt Fanny, I would not."

"Go on, my niece, I am ever so much better than when you commenced; another of your favourites, please."

Hattie thought for a moment and then went on:

> "I heard the voice of Jesus say,
> 'Come unto Me and rest;
> Lay down, thou weary one, lay down
> Thy head upon My breast.'
>
> "I came to Jesus as I was,
> Weary, and worn, and sad;
> I found in Him a resting place,
> And He has made me glad."

"Do you like that, Hattie?"

"Indeed I do, Aunt Fanny, like it ever so much. And that childish one, 'the Sweet Story of Old,' which says:

" I wish that His hands had been placed on my head,
    That His arms had been thrown around me."

"I am very fond of that, too, babyish though
it may be."

Miss Wood smiled. "You have missed one, Hattie, that is a great favourite with you, I know.
A sweet, quaint old hymn."

" Oh, yes—"

" Are you too tired to sing it ?"

" Not just that one."

> " Art thou weary, art thou languid,
>   Art thou sore distrest ?
> Come to Me, saith One and coming
>   Be at rest !
>
> " Hath He marks to lead me to Him,
>   If He be my guide ?
> In His feet and hands are wound prints
>   And His side.
>
> " Hath He diadem as Monarch
>   That His brow adorns ?
> Yea, a crown, in very surety,
>   But of thorns.
>
> " If I find Him, if I follow,
>   What His guerdon here ?
> Many a sorrow, many a labour,
>   Many a tear.

" If I still hold closely to Him,
    What hath He at last ?
Sorrow vanquished, labour ended,
                Jordan past.

" If I ask Him to receive me,
    Will He say me nay ?
Not till earth and not till Heaven˙
                Pass away.

" Finding, following, keeping, struggling,
    Is He sure to bless ?
Angels, martyrs, prophets, virgins,
                Answer, Yes !"

A good night's rest restored Miss Wood to her
usual healthy condition. Hattie tried in vain to
get into her aunt's study ; that lady positively refused to open the door. In the afternoon, however, she was in the parlour, with a large basket
of fancy work beside her. Hattie joyfully
pounced upon her elderly relative. " Aunt Fanny
are you very busy ? "

" Don't you see that I am ? "

" I want you to do something for me."

" Go to a Temperance meeting, I'll warrant ! "

" No, Aunt Fanny ; it's some writing."

" Writing !" and the old maid gazed at her

niece through her spectacles ; " what in the world is it you want ? "

" Oh, just to publish a little leaflet-book, suitable for enclosing letters—like *these*—" and she shewed her aunt some that were published by the Women's National Christian Temperance Union in the States.

" And you wish me to write it for you. Why not do it yourself ? "

" Because I cannot."

" Nonsense, you have written essays at school."

" Yes; but that is a very different thing. The mere thought of preparing matter for the press makes me feel nervous."

The old maid laughed heartily. " I'll do it for you, Hattie. What is the subject ? "

" That model Temperance meeting ! I want a full account of it to publish in the form of a little book."

Miss Wood smiled. " You are anxious that Mr. Rose's admirable chairmanship should do good to other Temperance societies. Where do you intend to send the leaflets—to your friends in Canada and Prince Edward Island ? "

" Yes; and to those in the United States and
England and Australia as well. Mr. Rose's words
cannot fail to be a blessing to them all."

" You will have to ask his permission."

" Indeed I won't—" and Hattie's look of per-
plexity made the spinster laugh.

" Why not ? "

" Because he might growl."

" I would not care if he did. But please yourself, my niece ; it is not absolutely necessary to ask
him."

" I don't think so, either. That meeting was
public property. Here is the account. Please
write it over again and make it fit for the press."

" Very well ; you had better put the paper on
my desk, Hattie."

Mrs. Somerville immediately obeyed ; and it
was not long before Miss Wood found the time
to prepare the required document.

A week or so afterwards, when Hattie returned
from the Division, she pressed her aunt to come
on the next Tuesday and join too.

" Why, have you had such an extra good time
to-night ? What was going on ? " questioned the
spinster.

"Coldstream Division paid us a fraternal visit, Aunt Fanny; and we had a very pleasant evening."

"Cannot I hear something of it, though I am not a member?" inquired Miss Wood. "Tell me all about the entertainment part of the meeting; there is nothing secret in that."

"I believe not. The Worthy Patriarch, Brother Dilworth, welcomed the members from 'Coldstream,' and one of their number replied in a short address. A visiting brother from Oshawa also said a few words, reporting that the Division there was in a languishing state. During the evening, Brother Daniel Rose gave a very touching reading, entitled 'Save the Boy,' and a number of songs were sung both by brothers and sisters."

"And what of Mr. George M. Rose?" snapped the old maid.

"Oh, I'm coming to him; never fear! He gave us a Temperance address—"

"Which was the best part of the evening's enjoyment?"

"Yes; it was. Brother G. M. Rose referred to

a song which had just been sung, viz: 'Annie Laurie,' and said that it would find an echo in the heart of every man who had ever loved a woman. He related a touching incident of the Crimean war, which took place during the storming of the Redan. One afternoon, the soldiers, who were wearied with the continual cannonading of the place, had a short respite. A song was proposed, and immediately ·'Annie Laurie' went all along the line. The English, Scotch and Irish regiments took it up in succession. No matter what was his nationality, each man thought of his own 'Annie Laurie,' and the words exactly fitted every case. The song had an inspiring influence; the cannonading re-commenced, and that night was signalized by the capture of the Redan. There was great loss of life, and many an 'Annie Laurie' had to mourn the loss of her lover. Mr. Rose said that a little thing had happened that afternoon which had pleased and encouraged him greatly, and which he regarded as quite providential. He is a member of the Board of Trade, and a meeting was to be held at three o'clock, but he had forgotten all about it until half an hour past

the time, when a member came in and insisted
most urgently that he should immediately accompany him to the place. They had no sooner
arrived there than a brewer took the floor, and
moved that the Board of Trade request the Dominion Board to petition the Government to reduce
the duty on malt. Mr. Rose at once inquired,
' what interest it was that we were asked to protect.'

" ' The farmers,' replied the brewer.

" ' Oh, you're very kind to the farmers!' said
Mr. Rose, with cutting sarcasm. 'But *I'm here
to protect another interest—that of the people!*'
Some discussion followed. The brewer found
he had more than one teetotaller to contend
against and quietly withdrew his motion. His
giving in amused Mr. Rose, because that same
man had fought like a devil in the Dunkin Bill
contest. The idea of making liquor any cheaper
than at present, was strenuously opposed by the
speaker. He mentioned the dire effects which
followed the reduction in the price of licenses for
the sale of malt liquors in England, when nearly
every third dwelling was converted into a beer-

house. The cry that was raised about taxing the poor man's beer was a perfect fallacy ; the money now spent on liquor could be saved and employed to far greater advantage. Mr. Rose was very unwilling that the members of the Board of Trade should commit themselves to any such thing as the reduction of the duty on malt. "Let the brewers go to Ottawa themselves and petition for it," said he. He very justly regarded it as providential, that he was brought to the meeting in time to defeat the schemes of the liquor men. As for Oshawa Division, (alluding to some remarks made by the member of that Division) he was sorry that it was in a declining state. There were too many great men in it—for instance, J. S. Larke, who was becoming noted in politics, and Edward Carswell, whose oratory had swayed the people of Canada. Such men thought the Division too small for their exertions, and the consequence was that Oshawa, which was once the Banner Division, was suffered to go down and now occupied an insignificant place. The great men of Crystal Fountain Division, on the contrary, always stood firm and true to the Order, and their Division was in a most flourish-

ing condition. We had another contest before us
this winter. One of to-day's papers gave notice
that a lecturer was going throughout the Province
to convince the people that all Temperance legis-
lation was of no avail, and that the true method
was to button-hole people on the street and thus
convert them to the cause. Mr. Rose said that
such persons forgot that there are men in our city,
whom even the grace of God can scarcely save—
men, who must be protected from themselves.
He expressed his pleasure at the way in which
Coldstream Division had turned out to meet us,
and hoped that during the winter many evenings
might be spent in a similar manner. Sometimes
we might have a discussion as to the best method
of promoting the cause. We were all called
'brothers' in our rituals ; but if we did not know
one another when we met on the streets and in
the market, how could we be brothers ? These
fraternal visits were the means of our getting acquainted. If the brethren from 'Coldstream'
could tell us how to become better Sons of Temperance ; how to do more for the cause; we would
listen to them gladly and take their advice."

The old maid looked keenly at her niece. "You have done well to remember all that," she said. " Now, I hope you'll profit by it."

" The same to yourself, Aunt Fanny." ·

" Go on and finish that account, you impertinent thing."

"After Mr. Rose's speech we had some more singing. Mr. Cameron made a few remarks concerning Temperance, and moved a vote of thanks to the members of Coldstream Division. Mr. Rose seconded it, quoting the lines,

' Better loved they canna be—
Surely they'll come back again.'

And soon afterwards the Division closed."

" Doubtless you enjoyed the evening very much. Hattie," she added suddenly, " You were mistaken in saying you had not seen Mr. Rose act as chairman at the meeting of a Reform Club before."

" I meant in the Albert Hall, Aunt Fanny ; and had forgotten the excursion of the clubs from up north, to Victoria Park. He was chairman, then, and right glad I was of it."

"Of course, because you wanted those moral suasionists to have some Prohibition hammered into them, and thought that Mr. Rose was just the man to do it."

Mrs. Somerville laughed. "Well, I thought about right," she said.

The spinster gave her spectacles a vigorous rub, as she remarked, " He shall never hammer it into me."

"Don't you be too sure, Aunt Fanny; I cannot agree with you there. Are you going to bed ? Good night."

CHAPTER XVI.

THE " LITTLE GEMS."

"HATTIE, your friend, Matilda Harding, is in distress ;" and Miss Wood set down her cup of coffee and looked gravely at her niece.

" What is the matter ? "

" Her husband has failed."

Hattie's knife dropped from her hand.

" Be careful of that china plate or you will have to buy me another," said the spinster, ominously shaking her head.

Mrs. Somerville looked blankly at her relative and remarked in dismay, " It does not seem possible, Aunt Fanny. I thought that Tom was soon going to retire."

L

"He never will now. There is nothing for it but to commence life afresh."

"How did it happen?"

"Why, he was involved with a firm on the other side of the line, and apparently thought it as solid as the world's foundations, but it has gone under, and Mr. Harding with it. They have lost everything. You need not look so grieved, my niece; thay have no children and are comparatively young, both being under forty. Tom has energy and perseverance; he will soon regain his lost position."

"Indeed, I hope so; it will be very hard for Matilda, who is more like a wax doll than a woman."

"So far as finery is concerned, that is, unfortunately, too true. Mr. Harding has acted very honourably and given up everything to his creditors; they will not lose a cent, I believe."

"Aunt Fanny, what has become of that beautiful home? Matilda was so proud of it."

"Why, Hattie, it passed into the hands of his drincipal creditor. I knew you would take this to heart," continued Miss Wood, "and therefore kept it from you as long as possible. I was obliged to tell you now, for Matilda is coming here to-day, and you must try to comfort her."

" Is she in great distress ?"

." Yes, but it is not the loss of her wealth that has caused such trouble of mind. I tried to find out but altogether failed."

Matilda came according to promise. She was evidently comforted by the sympathy of her friends, but there was something the matter which they could not understand. Hattie gently inquired what it was.

" Oh, it was not Tom's fault," said Mrs. Harding; " it was all a judgment on me, because I would not listen to Mr. Rose !"

Hattie could not help smiling.

" You are very unfeeling," remarked Miss Wood to her niece; then turning to Matilda, " What could Mr. Rose have to do with it, my dear ?"

" Why, I would not listen to him, ma'am, though conscience loudly told me that he was right. Look att'he noble life he has lived ! Tom as often told me about it, for my husband is as

ardent an admirer of Mr. Rose as you would wish
to see. Miss Wood, during all these years I have
often been impressed by sermons, by Tom's example, and lots of other things. They urged me
to do differently, but in vain; and I verily believe that those speeches of Mr. Rose were my
last chance. You know how his life gives force
and vehemence to his words, so earnest—so devoted, so true to everything that is good. Hattie,
that life and those words were my last chance ;
God will not give me another."

" Oh, Matilda, do not speak so—"

" I don't mean that He will not save me if I
repent," said Mrs. Harding sadly. " I hope He
will ; but I can never expect to do any good
now, for my life is a perfect wreck."

" Is that what you mean ? " returned Mrs. Somerville eagerly. " I can give you some comfort, or
rather——" and she took down a book from the
library and began to turn over the leaves.

The spinster looked keenly at her niece.

" Matilda, you will not think anything of my
opinion," continued Hattie; " but, I presume, you
will believe Mr. Rose."

" Did *he* write that book ?" snapped Miss Wood.

" He is the editor of it, Aunt Fanny, and selected all the pieces it contains."

" I'll just look it carefully over," grimly remarked the spinster, " and criticise his taste, so I will."

Mrs. Somerville laughed. " There are two volumes, Aunt Fanny. They are called 'Readings, Recitations and Diologues,' and contain nothing but pure gold. Criticise as much as you please, I assure you they will bear it. The American 'Temperance Speakers,' etc., are good, but Mr. Rose's little gems beat them out and out."

" They seem to be beautifully got up, at all events," remarked Miss Wood, peevishly, as she keenly eyed the volume in the hand of her niece.

" Of course, because they are the work of his firm. Those little books are admirably adapted for all manner of Temperance Societies, whether they be Divisions, Lodges, Clubs, or what not."

" And, doubtless, have helped greatly to spread Total Abstinence and Prohibition principles

through the country. Now read those lines to
Matilda, if you have found them."

Hattie immediately commenced—

ALL HAVE GOT THEIR WORK TO DO.

" Why these murmurs and repinings ?
　Who can alter what is done ?
See the future brightly shining ;
　There are goals yet to be won.
Grieving is at best a folly,
　Oftentimes it is a sin ;

When we see a glaring error,
　We should a reform begin ;
We should all be up and stirring,
　With determination true ;
Young and old men, rich and poor men,
　All have got their work to do."

Matilda's face brightened. " Mr. Rose evidently thinks there is a chance for every one to
work," she said. " Thank you for reading that,
Hattie; I will try to do better for the future."

" My niece, there is something in those lines
that you ought to take to yourself."

" What is it ? "

" When you see a glaring error,
　You should a reform begin."

" Oh, so I do, Aunt Fanny."

" Indeed, I'm glad to hear it," returned Miss Wood.

Towards evening Matilda departed, and Ronald arrived.

" It is very cold and stormy. I am not going out to-night," said the spinster, decidedly.

" But this is the 21st of December, and there is a special Concert of the Club," remonstrated Hattie ; " you have not been present since Mr. Rose was chairman."

" No ; that was only two weeks ago, and I heard enough Temperance to last me for a month. His name is on the programme, and I'll not go—so, there's an end of it."

• When Hattie returned home, Miss Wood laid aside her manuscript, and asked for an account of the meeting.

" I'll tell you what I can remember," said Mrs. Somerville. " When the time came for opening, Mr. Rose took the chair and read the hymn, 'All hail the power of Jesus' name.' (Aunt Fanny, no one reads that hymn so beautifully as he does.) It was then sung by the choir and audience. Mr. Rose came forward to the front of the platform,

and stated that owing to the unavoidable absence
of Mr. Howland, the Club had called upon him
to take the chair.   It was unnecessary to name
the objects of the Association, for they were already well known.   The primary one was to get .
people to sign the total abstinence Pledge, and
the secretary was ready to take down the names
of any who would unite with us.   But our principal object to-night, was to obtain funds to carry
on the work.   Mr. Rose went on to say that Temperance people were always accused of being
stingy, and proceeded to account for it by alluding to the obvious fact of a drinking man spend-
ing all his money in the tavern, thus supporting
the children of other people who would care
nothing for him in his time of need.   When such
a person left the saloon and became a Temperance
man, he would devote his earnings to the comfort of his wife and family, which was right ; but
in many cases he would go to the extreme point
and become stingy.   Mr. Rose advocated a middle
course : he did not like Temperance people to be
stingy.   Among those present were ladies who
had braved the storm.   Were the men becoming

effeminate ?—(Aunt Fanny, Mr. Rose ought not to have been out such a night as this : he has a very bad cold, and will be laid up entirely, I'm afraid, if he does not take better, care of himself. He came down in this snow-storm, all the way from Clover Hill, and there is not the slightest excuse for the others who were absent.)—Mr. Rose went on to say that those who were present to give their support to the Club, were persons who had not been bitten by the serpent at all. Members who have been benefited by the institution, were not here, but *ought* to have been. Mr. Rose said he was in a scolding mood to-night—his remarks were not intended for those who were present—' but,' he emphatically added, ' give my compliments to those who are absent, and tell them they ought to be ashamed of themselves.' "

" Go on, my niece. What are you waiting for ?" asked Miss Wood, grimly.

" To give you time to take that message to yourself, Aunt Fanny. Living in the central part of the city, there is no excuse for you. Allow me to give you Mr. Rose's compliments, and also to tell you that you ought to be ashamed of yourself !"

"It will be a month of Mondays, Hattie, before I go again!" angrily exclaimed Miss Wood.

"Nothing of the kind, Aunt Fanny. You shall go next Saturday, or I am very much mistaken."

"Can you remember any more?" coldly inquired the spinster.

"After the chairman's address, there were songs, and so forth. One was sung by a little boy, who was only four years of age. Mr. Rose took him by the hand and led him to the front of the platform, saying 'I'm going to introduce the youngest member of the Club, with the exception of one of my own babies.' (Aunt Fanny, Mr. Rose must have meant that little darling of his, with the curly golden hair, like its father's.)"

"I don't care what he meant," snapped the spinster; "go on, I say."

"The child did well and pleased the audience. More songs followed; and towards the close of the meeting Mr. Rose came forward and said a few words."

"And aren't you going to tell me?" asked Miss Wood in surprise, as her niece stopped short.

"I was only thinking, Aunt Fanny, so as to

give you as nearly as possible his exact words.
After some remarks about Temperance in general,
Mr. Rose said, 'And now, members of the Club, a
word to you. The holiday season is coming on
Next week will be Christmas and the week after,
New Year's—' and he went on to caution them
to keep their pledge. ·Ladies who were members
of the Club he need not speak to, but those who
were not, he entreated not to offer liquor to
their friends. They might tempt some member
who had been struggling for weeks to stand,
and perhaps cause him to break his pledge. '*The
sin of his fall shall be on your head* !' emphatically added Mr. Rose. He then again warned the
reformed men to '*Stand firm—dare to do right* ;
and if any ask you to drink, I don't say "knock
them down," but if it's a lady, kiss her: she'll prefer that !'"

" Shocking—shocking !" exclaimed the spinster.
" Oh, Hattie, how can you possibly laugh at
such a thing ? I am astonished that——"

" Why, Aunt Fanny, you know, as well as I
do, that Mr. Rose was only in play." So saying,
Mrs. Somerville took her "Sacred Songs and Solos,"
and departed, leaving her relative in peace.

On the Monday before Christmas, when Miss Wood and her niece were engaged in earnest conversation, Mr. McFarlane entered.

" We were discussing the future prospects of the Club, in view of the approaching election of officers ;" remarked the spinster. " Hattie laments that Mr. Rose cannot take the Presidency. Now, I am glad, that he has not the time to devote to it, otherwise he would make us all Prohibitionists. Beside that, he would punish reformed men who broke their pledge, by keeping them out of office until they could behave better."

" And very rightly," answered Mrs. Somerville.

" It is no use talking, my niece. He is not the man for such a position—in fact, is so hard, that I question very much if it would be possible to draw a tear out of him."

The Professor hastily replied, " You are altogether mistaken, madam. I have heard Mr. Rose say that ' he cries like a baby himself.' "

Miss Wood looked greatly amazed, while Hattie reddened, and angrily remarked, " It is only lately, Ronald, that you have become acquainted

with Mr. Rose, and must have heard him say that
to some one else. It is very dishonourable to re-
peat private conversation."

. "My dear, those words you are lecturing me
about were spoken on the deck of a steamboat
full of excursionists, and in the hearing of anyone who might chance to pass by."

"Oh, my niece is altogether too precise in her
notions of what is honourable and the reverse,"
answered Miss Wood. "I do not hesitate to
leave my most particular correspondence (relating
to women's rights, etc.,) in her way continually ;
she never dreams of meddling with it. But, Hattie, there are many things said, even in private
conversation that are not intended to be sedulous-
ly kept from everybody, and there is not the
slightest harm in repeating them. That statement of Ronald's is one. I confess I was mistaken in Mr. Rose. However excusable it may
be in women to shed tears—the strong-minded of
our sex are rarely guilty of such a thing—it is
an act of the greatest weakness in a man. To
acknowledge that he cries like a baby—well, Mr.
Rose ought to have been ashamed of himself !

Why, my niece, what is the matter ?   You look
as strangely at me as though I were saying something wicked."

"And so you are," replied Hattie earnestly.
" Aunt Fanny, you meant those words for Mr.
Rose, but you reflected just as much on our
Saviour. The only perfect man who trod our
earth, *cried*. Was it an act of the greatest weakness in Him ?   Ought Jesus to have been ashamed
of Himself ? "

" My niece, you are the most irreverent creature
that ever lived," exclaimed Miss Wood, who felt
shocked at such an application of her words.   " I
cannot conceive what there is in Mr. Rose that so
constantly reminds you of Christ ! "

"That is because you won't," returned Hattie.
" Ronald," she added suddenly, " are you sure that
Mr. Rose said those words ? "

Yes, my dear.   You don't consider it against
him, do you ? "

" Oh, no ; it is a great credit to him ; but——"

" But what, Hattie ? "

" I should never have thought it."

" I daresay not," said the Professor ; " and I can

tell you why. You have seen him on the platform more than anywhere else—"

"Ronald, I am sure that Mr. Rose has a warm
heart ; it takes no prophet to tell that."

" Very right, my dear. He is firm and true to
his principles at all times ; stern in rebuke of
wrong ; hot and fiery on the platform ; yet for
all that, Brother G. M. Rose has such a loving,
gentle, child-like nature, that I verily believe,
though you searched the world over, you would
not find such another. You may smile, Hattie, but
I am telling you the sober truth."

"Stop, stop, Ronald," exclaimed Miss Wood.
"You are just undoing my work. I have been
trying to persuade my niece that ' distance lends
enchantment to the view,' and so forth ; that if
she knew Mr. Rose, though ever so slightly, she
would speedily cease to hold him in such high
estimation."

"Miss Wood, how could you attempt to make
her believe such a falshood ? I defy any man,
woman or child to know Mr. Rose and not love
him !"

The old maid was too much provoked to reply.

Ronald went on. Those photographs you have, Hattie, represent Mr. Rose as he appears on the platform; I have brought you one which shews how he looks in daily life—" and he handed Mrs. Somerville a picture, which she gazed at long and earnestly.

"What makes you smile, Hattie?"

"Because, in this photograph, Mr. Rose looks so remarkably gentle!"

Ronald laughed. "You think of him as a red-hot Prohibitionist—"

"And so he is!"

"Yes; but this picture is just as true to life as any of yours can possibly be. Do you like it?"

"Oh, very much!"

"You'll like it in your own room," snapped the spinster, "for I won't have it here."

The Professor smiled as he inquired, "Well Hattie, have you forgiven me for repeating those few words?"

"I don't think it was right, Ronald."

"Indeed! I'm going to tell you something else—"

"I'll not listen."

" Don't, my dear, and I will just say it to your
Aunt. Miss Wood," turning to that lady, " on
the same boat, last summer, and on the same day,
Mr. Millar, who was then our Grand Worthy
Patriarch, tried to persuade Mr. Rose to make a
visit to Scotland—"

" Oh, Ronald, I do hope he won't go ! "

Mr. McFarlane laughed. " I thought you were
not going to listen, Hattie ! "

" I couldn't help it."

" My niece, how delightful it would be if
such a thing happened. He would probably be
away for three months at least. Aren't you
afraid that every Temperance society in the
Dominion would be dead and buried before he
got back ? "

" Ronald, go on and finish what you were saying," urged Hattie, impatiently.

" Very well. Mr. Millar coaxed his companion
to visit Scotland during the following year. Mr.
Rose replied in the determined tone that is so
characteristic of him, *I'll not go until we get
Prohibiton!* "

The old maid's countenance fell. " Then he

M

will wait for some time," she answered, with a sneer.

"Ronald, was Mr. Rose in earnest?" asked Mrs. Somerville eagerly.

"I believe so, Hattie, and is a blessing for the cause in Canada."

CHAPTER XVII.

"YE DID IT UNTO ME."

CHRISTMAS came and went. On the night of Friday, 27th December, Miss Wood was sitting in her study, when the street door opened, and a moment after, Hattie burst in upon her.

" Well, my niece, is the election of officers over? Whatever is the matter? I have rarely seen you look so angry and troubled."

" Aunt Fanny," answered Mrs. Somerville, her voice trembling with passion and excitement, "those reformed men have not a spark of gratitude in them—not a single one!"

" What have they done?" inquired the spinster in amazement.

" You remember how, at the last election, they

all wanted to put Mr. Rose in for President by
acclamation, which for good reasons he refused;
how they would not listen to his declining the
position of Treasurer; how when he arose to do
so they applauded in such a violent manner that
it was impossible for him to make himself heard.
You remember how he accepted it for the time,
until the Club which had just split in two, was
in a more settled state. Then he wished to give
it up, because he could not attend the Executive
meetings, and that Executive passed a resolution, *praying* him to retain the position of Treasurer, though unable to be present on Monday
evenings."

" I remember. Do be more calm, my niece.
Where is the good of losing your temper ? "

" Aunt Fanny, it is impossible to help it," bitterly returned Mrs. Somerville. " You know how
Mr. Rose kindly yielded to their entreaties and
retained the position. You know, too, that he
was the originator of this movement, and that those
reformed men, under God, owe their salvation to
Brother G. M. Rose. He has stuck to the Central
Club from first to last; all through its darkest

days, he gave it his countenance and support, when without him it would not have lived an hour. Aunt Fanny, I hardly believed that such wicked ingratitude existed in human nature, as they have shown towards him. Not the Club as a whole, for only thirty members took the trouble to attend—"

"Holiday time," remarked Miss Wood.

"Mr. Rose was absent at a festival of his Sunday School. He is the teacher of a large Bible Class, consisting of grown-up boys and girls, and could not possibly be with us. A majority of that hole-and-corner meeting turned him out of office and put a person in his place, who, to use a favourite expression of yours, is not fit to hold a candle to him. *There* are moral suasionists for you!" exclaimed Hattie, excitedly.

"My dear niece, do sit down and try to be more calm," said the spinster uneasily.

"Aunt Fanny, I can't be calm. Those men have shown themselves to be utterly vile. More heartless wretches I hope never to meet!"

"Hattie, you will injure yourself," said the old maid, who felt alarmed at the anger and excitement of her niece; "I shall hear no more to-night, go to your room and tell me the rest to-morrow."

It was dark on the following morning when Miss Wood awoke. "Actually that is Hattie pacing up and down," she thought to herself; "her step was the last thing I heard before going to sleep and it's the first on awaking. I wonder if she went to bed at all."

Soon there came a knock at her door which was securely locked, and a voice outside said, "Aunt Fanny!"

"Get away with your Aunt Fannies!" screamed the spinster, raising herself on her elbow. "I wish every member of that Central Club was at the bottom of the sea, and you too. I'm not going to get up yet. What time is it?"

"Half-past four."

"Just go back to your room," answered Miss Wood, who felt annoyed at being disturbed so early.

Mrs. Somerville retreated, while the spinster gave her pillow two or three vigorous thumps by way of a shake, and settled herself to sleep again. At breakfast she was relieved to find that her niece had cooled down considerably.

" Hattie, do drink your coffee; were you awake all the night ? "

" Oh, no."

" Did you cry ? "

" Cry ! I wish I could, Aunt Fanny ; did *you* never feel so bitter and hard and angry, that crying was impossible ; I am in that *happy* condition now."

Miss Wood looked anxiously at her niece. " My dear, you should read the ' Sermon on the Mount ;' ' Love your enemies, etc.'"

" I know it by heart."

" Indeed, I greatly doubt if it ever got further than your head."

No answer.

" Did those who voted against Mr. Rose give any reason for their disgraceful conduct ? Had they any fault to find with him ? "

" Fault ! " echoed Hattie in astonishment ; "not the shadow of one."

" Then, it was spite-work, and will return on their own heads."

" I hope it will, Aunt Fanny. If that clique have acted fairly and honourably by Brother

Rose, let them rejoice in their new treasurer and let him rejoice in them ; but, if not——"

"Don't finish that, Hattie. You had better not wish shame and disgrace upon them, though they richly deserve it."

"Then you will allow me to say of those heart-less men, what St. Paul said of an opponent who had done him much evil, 'The Lord reward them according to their works.'"

"My niece, considering the wicked way in which they have acted, those words are equival-ent to a curse."

"Well, don't you think St. Paul meant them as such ? I'm in good company ;" bitterly returned Hattie.

The old maid felt both troubled and perplexed. She was really fond of her niece, indeed cared more for her than for all the clubs in existence, though she took good heed never to allow Hattie to suspect such a thing. "What a hard, stony look, she has," thought the spinster, anxiously. "I would take her to a revival meeting to-mor-row. But no revival meeting that I ever saw, had the slightest effect upon Hattie. My unfortunate niece is no Methodist. What to do with her I don't know."

When evening came Miss Wood remarked, "I'm going to the meeting. There will be no danger of any Prohibition to-night."

" I have lost all interest in the Club," coldly returned Mrs. Somerville.

" And in the cause ? "

" Oh, no! That is a very different thing."

" Well, come with me now at all events. Mr. Rose is not likely to be there ; he will doubtless have nothing more to do with a Club that has treated him so badly. There are so many other Temperance societies with which he is connected, · and the Club will find plenty of work."

It was with extreme reluctance that Mrs. Somerville accompanied her aunt to the Albert Hall. To their surprise Mr. Rose was present.

The chair was taken by Mr. T. H. McConkey, and his address was followed by songs and readings as usual. Then he asked " one to come forward who had always something good for us, and whom we all liked to hear ; he would call upon a Prohibitionist, Brother Rose."

Mr. G. M. Rose went up on the platform and said,
" Ladies and gentlemen, *I'm a Prohibitionist.*"
And he proceeded most earnestly to advocate the
entire up-rooting of the liquor traffic. He advised us to go on with moral suasion as well,
but never to rest satisfied with that alone. If
he could get the Parliament to pass a Prohibitory
law to-morrow, he would not do it, because the
country was not ready for such a measure; the people must be educated up to it. He then added
emphatically, *"I want every member of this Club
to be a Prohibitionist!"* Mr. Rose said that he had
come here for something else—to give his valedictory. While he was at the Sunday School festival last night, it being impossible for him to be
in two places at once, the election had been held
and they had put him out of office. When he
saw it in the paper this morning he could hardly
believe it. What had he done to deserve cen-
sure? What crime had he been guilty of? He
said he would tell them now, that when bills had
come in and there was no money in the Treasury,
he had paid them himself, rather than allow the
credit of the Club to suffer. He was glad to be

able to tell them that their financial position was pretty good. It was evident that Mr. Rose felt deeply wounded by the manner in which he had been treated. When he saw the list of officers in the paper that morning, he knew that it was meant as an insult to G. M. Rose. One reason for his expulsion was that he was a Prohibitionist, and went further than many of them were prepared to do ; another was because of his religious views. He did not believe that man was totally depraved, there was always some good in him, " a little bit of God in him, so to speak;" and if we could touch that spot, we could set him on his feet and make a man of him again. Mr. Rose stated that if he had not been independent in his views he would not have stood in this position to night. His voice was tremulous and there were tears in his eyes as he said, "I never thought the day would come when G. M. Rose should be put out of that Executive." He nobly added, that he would not leave the Club, but work hard for it, and watch those men who had acted in such a manner, and if they did not do their duty they should be turned out of office. He said that

his father was a poor working man, who never
earned more than ten shillings a week as long as
he lived ; but he had brought up his children re-
spectably, and the mother had done all in her
power to give them a good education. He and his
brothers and sisters had been Temperance from
their youth. If the Club went down it would
make no difference to him—would not affect his
principles,—" *For G. M. Rose had sworn to be a
teetotaller.*"

The speaker had the heart sympathy of his
audience, and the clique who had voted against
him looked thoroughly ashamed.

Miss Wood was greatly relieved when she saw
tears in the eyes of her niece. On reaching
home, Hattie's overwrought feelings gave way in
a passion of grief. The spinster was at her wit's
end ; she vainly wished for Ronald, but he was
away in Roseville. At length she said coaxingly,
" My dear child, do not distress yourself so. It
cannot be prevented now."

. " Oh, Aunt Fanny," answered Hattie, with a
sob, " I did not think that they had hurt Mr.
Rose so much. He could scarcely help crying
himself."

" Scarcely !" echoed the old maid. "Why, when he came down from the platform, after giving that valedictory, and took a seat among the audience, he put his head down on his hand, and more than once wiped the tears of his face with his handkerchief."

" Oh, Aunt Fanny, I am glad I did not know that."

" And so am I," grimly responded Miss Wood. " I was afraid you would turn your head, Hattie. Mr. Rose was sitting so near you, that, had you known he was crying, it would almost have broken your heart. You were miserable enough in all conscience as it was. Now, for my part, I was really provoked, and putting on my spectacles scowled horribly at those who had the least thing to do with the disgraceful affair. Where's the good of feelingly so badly, my niece? It won't hurt."

" What ?"

" You're a stupid thing, Hattie, and your brain must be bewildered," impatiently returned the spinster. "I meant," she continued in a sarcastic tone, " that it would not hurt Mr. Rose to

shed those precious tears, as you doubtless think
them.   Now, don't get angry.   There's another
thing, you always keep poking texts of scripture
in my face, so here's one for you.   'All things
work together for good to them that love God.'
Of course, that is not true; those words don't
mean anything and never will be fulfilled."

" Yes, they are true; they do mean something,
and will be fulfilled to the letter," excitedly
answered Hattie.   " You thought that Mr. Rose
would leave that ungrateful Club to its fate and
never come near it again.   So did I. But instead
of that——"

" My dear niece, it is useless to grieve over it
now."

"I cannot help it.   Whether in that Grand
Division or elsewhere, Mr. Rose never looked so
noble as he did to-night.   Is he not a better Christian, a thousand times over, a better Christian
than those who voted him out ?"

"I have not the slightest doubt of it."

" Nor I.   That new treasurer and his companions may think themselves honoured to sit at
Mr. Rose's feet, both in this world and in the next."

"Unless they greatly alter their conduct, Hattie, I fear they will never have the chance." So saying, Miss Wood took up her family Bible and inquired, "What chapter shall I read to-night? Have you any choice?"

"Yes; please read the account of St. Paul's conversion, where the Lord appears to him and says, 'I am Jesus of Nazareth, whom thou persecutest.'"

Miss Wood was a little surprised, but she immediately turned to the wished-for portion of Scripture and read it aloud to her niece. Then she said coaxingly, "Take back those words that you spoke in anger, yesterday: 'The Lord reward them according to their works.'"

Mrs. Somerville raised her head. "I take the evil wish back: they will have enough to bear without it. Those persons little thought when they insulted Brother G. M. Rose, that they insulted every intelligent man in the community. But they *did*."

"If that be so, they will bitterly repent it."

"Of course it is so. Christ knew what it was not to be appreciated by those to whom He had done nothing but kindness. 'He came unto His own, and His own received Him not.' Up in heaven He may be, but He is the same yesterday, to-day and forever. Can you doubt that He took that insult to His younger brother as though it were done to Himself."

" I do not doubt it at all," said Miss Wood, who had been musing on the verses she had just read.

"Aunt Fanny, it is a comfort to know that Jesus loves and appreciates Mr. Rose. *He* counted those precious tears."

" Hattie, you will persist in taking my words in earnest," peevishly responded the old maid.

Her niece paid no attention to the remark, but went on, "He is a red-hot Prohibitionist, every inch of him; but for all that it is as Ronald said. Mr. Rose has a gentle, loving, child-like nature, and—so had Christ."

"Hattie, you deserve what you don't get."

" For speaking the truth ? Jesus sternly rebuked the hypocritical Scribes and Pharisees, in His character of Reformer; but He also wept with the sisters of Lazarus and even over the wicked city of Jerusalem."

The spinster saw that she had no alternative but to give up the point. After a pause, she inquired, " My niece, do you forgive Mr. Thompson and those other persons ?"

" I'll *try;* but it is impossible either to like or respect them. I hope their consciences will give them no peace, and that they will never know a day's happiness until they go down on their knees to Brother G. M. Rose and humbly ask his forgiveness."

The old maid laughed. " I will not ask you to take that back, Hattie ; it is right enough. By all means, tell those parties your truly amiable wish concerning them."

" Certainly ; you may depend upon that."

CHAPTER XVIII.

THE GOSPEL OF JOHN.

" I MUST try to take the mind of my niece off all unpleasant subjects, this Sabbath morning," thought Miss Wood to herself. " Hattie," she remarked, as soon as breakfast was over, "I have the synopsis of a sermon here, which I particularly wish you to study at once ; you can master the principal points before church-time."

" It is a good antidote to some of Mr. Greg's teachings," explained the spinster, seeing that Mrs. Somerville looked surprised.

" What is the subject ? "

" The Deity of Christ."

" I will read it carefully, Aunt Fanny; but will not next Sunday answer your purpose ? "

" No ; you must begin immediately," returned
Miss Wood, as she handed a long slip of paper to
her niece. " Those paragraphs that are marked,
you must read aloud to me, and then study the
whole thing carefully for yourself. It is by the
Rev. Wm. Taylor, D.D., of New York. Now commence," and the old maid settled herself in her
easy chair, in an attitude of close attention.

Hattie saw there was no escape, so she took the
slip and began to read.

" And the Word was made flesh and dwelt
among us, and we beheld His glory, the glory as
of the only begotten of the Father, full of grace
and truth." . . . First, the person spoken of
was called the Word. Much had been written by
learned authors on the Logos, or Word, and different opinions expressed and maintained. Which
of these was correct was not of much importance in
the present discourse, but in looking at the context
of the subject, three things could be discovered.
First, that the Word was God ; second, that
He was distinct, that He was with God ; and,
third, that He was the Creator of the universe.
It was impossible to have a stronger assertion of

His deity than this. . . . They would be
wrong if they thought the Word of God began
with the birth of Christ. 'All things were made
by Him, and without Him was not anything
made that was made.' . . . In the second
place was the affirmation regarding the Word.
He was made flesh, or more literally translated,
He became flesh. That was the manner in which
John spoke of the truth of Christ. . . . The
one great miracle was the incarnation. However
mysterious in itself, it explained everything else
in the Bible. If the Word was God, and became
flesh, all was plain. If there was no incarnation,
there could be no Gospel for poor humanity; and
man might, indeed, despair of salvation, and there
was no use disputing any more about it. What
did it mean when it said that the Word became
flesh ? Not that He ceased to be God, but that
He became man, that through His humanity He
might give a manifestation of God. He took not
simply a human body, but took a human nature
into union with His deity. If they asked how
that could be possible, he must simply answer
that he could not explain, any more than he could

explain how his soul of which he was conscious,
remained in connection with his body. . . .
John is to speak of the glory of the Word made
flesh. The person of Christ was the great theme
of the writer, and each chapter had its own place
in the elaboration of the argument. In the first
chapter He is produced as the Lamb of God, in the
second, the temple of God, in the third, the glorious anti-type of the brazen serpent, in the fourth,
He said simply, 'I am,' in the fifth, He was judge
of all, in the sixth, the light, the good shepherd,
the truth, and the resurrection ———"

"Well, why do you stop ?"

"Because the reverend gentleman has quoted
the wrong chapters."

" I don't believe it."

"You shall soon be convinced. In the *eighth*
chapter, Jesus says 'I am ;' in the eighth and
ninth, He calls Himself the ' light of the world ; '
in the tenth, the ' good shepherd ;' in the eleventh,
the ' resurrection ; ' and in the fourteenth, the
' truth '—' I am the way, the truth, and the life —'"

"You are a fault-finding, criticising thing,
Hattie," said the old maid, in a tone of annoy-

ance. " If you had a good deal more of the Bible
in your heart and less in your head, it would be
vastly better. Go on, I say."

" And in further successive chapters, He
was represented as the King of Zion riding
in state into His capital ; the great intercessor, the
king of a spiritual dominion, the Lamb of God
sacrificed ; and last, the Resurrection and the
Life."

" Hattie, you have often read the gospel of St.
John, but did you ever read it as a whole, regarding the different chapters as so many links in one
chain."

" No, Aunt Fanny, but I intend to do so, now."

" Very well, go on."

"This gospel was above all others the gospel of
' I ams.' ·Was there ever such argument ? . .
Christ's Godhead was nowhere shown as in the
divine egotisms which were here showed to have
been uttered by Him, a being having about him
the inherent weakness of a man. No man having no higher nature than his manhood could
have spoken the words which Christ did. If
simply a man, He must have been either a fan-

atic or a madman ; but the fabric of His discourses proved that He who spoke them was not a blinded bigot, and the tenor of His arguments prove Him to have been perfectly sane in the prayer He makes. Even at the very throne of grace He says that for men to know Him was necessary to their salvation. . . . . That which a man clings to in the hour of danger must be stronger than himself, for if a sailor in a storm should cling to his ship-mate both would inevitably be swept from the deck by the rushing and irresistible waters. The mariner laid fast hold of the staunch bulwarks of the vessel, and was brought through in safety, and it was to the knowledge of the Godhead of Christ that man should cling. The reality of Christ's humanity assured mankind of ready sympathy at His hands. He was a man and knew a man's heart ; and though He had ascended on high, He was still the same Jesus as the angels described Him—a Saviour . . . Man was in sympathy with the fatherhood of God through the brotherhood of Christ. The human nature of the Saviour made the love of God available to man."

"Aunt Fanny," asked Mrs. Somerville earnestly, "Do you think that if a Unitarian read the gospel of John, as a whole, carefully following the argument throughout, that he would be convinced of the Deity of Christ?"

"I neither think nor care anything about it, Hattie."

There was silence for some minutes.

"I hope that there are no Unitarians in the clubs or other Temperance societies which my niece is in the habit of frequenting;" thought the spinster to herself. Then speaking aloud, she desired Hattie to make the most of her time and fix in her memory the leading points of the sermon, as they must soon get ready for church.

Half an hour passed very quietly.

Miss Wood looked up and suddenly inquired, "My niece, did the doctrine of the Trinity ever give you any trouble?"

"No, Aunt Fanny," answered Hattie, simply, "and because of the reason given by Dr. Taylor. The doctrine of the Trinity is no more of a mystery to me, no more difficult to believe, than that the

union of soul and body make one man—for instance, our beloved Mr. Rose."

"I do wish you would let Mr. Rose alone,"
grimly returned Miss Wood. "Here have I been
trying to keep unpleasant things from your
mind; and this is the result of it. I believe
you have been thinking of him the whole morning."

"Oh, Aunt Fanny, how is it possible to help
it, after his valedictory last night?"

"Go and get ready for church; I suppose you
won't come with me;" peevishly answered Miss
Wood.

On her return, the spinster duly questioned
her niece about the services, but obtained very
little satisfaction.

"You can scarcely tell me anything about
either the sermon or the text," crossly remarked
Miss Wood, "and I am convinced that your
thoughts must have been straying on Club matters all the time. What good did it do you to go
to church, I should like to know, when not a
blessed thing do you remember?"

"A verse of a hymn, which was sung fixed itself in my memory," replied Hattie in a low voice "it is so applicable to Mr. Rose."

"I'll warrant it," muttered the spinster; "your thoughts were busy about that miserable affair. Well, let me hear the verse."

"It seems like a comment on the text which you quoted last night, Aunt Fanny. 'All things work together for good to them that love God.'"

> "And good it is to bear the cross,
> And so Thy perfect peace to win;
> *And nought is ill, nor brings us loss.*
> *Nor works us harm,* save only—sin."

CHAPTER XIX.

"A MODEL HUSBAND."

"WHERE have you been to-night, Hattie," inquired Miss Wood.

"I was at the Executive meeting, The treasurer was to be there, you know. He was not present at the election of officers and consequently could not read his report. He did that to-night."

"Was he hot and angry?" enquired Miss Wood.

"Not in the least, but as good natured and gentle as he looks in that picture."

"Well, the club has had hard work to pull through the summer months, financially speaking," remarked the spinster. "Did the old Executive go out of office in debt?"

" Oh, no. The deficit was made up among themselves. Mr. Rose helped them; it is needless to tell you that."

" Indeed, I would not have given them a cent under the circumstances," emphatically replied Miss Wood. " I wonder if his ' coals of fire ' burned the heads of those persons who voted against him! Why don't you go on to quote the rest of the verse in Proverbs, Hattie, and tell me that ' the Lord shall reward him ?' "

" Because you know it very well yourself, Aunt Fanny. I am afraid," she added with a sigh, " that Brother Rose's standard of goodness and right is far higher than yours and mine."

" I don't care if it is;" snappishly returned Miss Wood.

On the following day she asked her niece to accompany her to do some shopping, which proved very tedious.

" Where are you going now ?"

" I want to show you the Albert Coffee House," replied Mrs. Somerville, as she opened the door.

Miss Wood mechanically followed. Hattie led her through the bar-room (an innocent kind of a

"bar," certainly, where only tea, coffee, etc., are
sold) and into the largest apartment, which is
used for meetings and purposes of amusement.

"This place has, doubtless, kept many a man
from going to the tavern," thoughtfully observed
the old maid. "I wonder who got it up."

"Aunt Fanny, don't you know?" asked Mrs.
Somerville in surprise.

"No, you need not try to make me believe that
Mr. Rose had anything to do with it."

"He had everything to do with it," emphatically replied Hattie. "Mr. Rose and Mr. Howland were the two gentlemen who (to use your
elegant expression) got it up." Why, I thought
every one in the city knew that. Come into this
room and see the library, and have a cup of
coffee."

Miss Wood followed her niece, who had often
been there before.

"I am going to look over those books," she remarked. "It was a good plan to have a reading-
room in connection with such an establishment.
You are tired, Hattie; sit down and drink your
coffee."

Soon Miss Wood read aloud, from the fly-leaf of one of the volumes in her hand, " To the Albert Club, from G. M. Rose." "Did you know that that name was in a number of those books, my niece ?"

" Yes, Aunt Fanny, I have often looked them over and admired that writing."

" Don't you wish you had just such an autograph ? "

" Oh, I have ; Ronald gave me one."

" Then you did not show it to me," growled the spinster. " I suppose you thought that I would tear it. Have you got one of Francis Murphy's ?"

" Yes, his name and address on a pledge card. It is only in pencil-writing, in a bold hand."

" I'll not hurt that, for he is a good moral suasionist ; but if I ever come across Edward Carswell's or——"

" I have three of his," replied Mrs. Somerville, eagerly, " but they are safely out of your reach."

Miss Wood scowled on her niece ; then coming to the table, she drank her coffee and broke off a small piece of the roll, to " see if it was light."

" Aren't they good, Aunt Fanny ? Is it not a boon to a working man to be able to get a cup of coffee and a buttered roll for five cents? The other articles of food are equally cheap in proportion."

" Indeed it is, Hattie."

" The same gentlemen who established this coffee-house, with its neat rooms and pretty mottoes on the walls, have just opened another on a larger scale. Such places ought to do an incalculable amount of good."

In the evening as Miss Wood sat intently gazing at the fire, her niece inquired, " What can you be thinking of, Aunt Fanny? It is rare indeed to see you go off into dream-land."

The old maid awakened from her reverie with a start. " Hattie," she said, " this is New-Year's Eve. That father of yours has spoiled you all your life and persists in doing so still. I want to get you something as a gift; but it seems useless, for he supplies every possible need, and gratifies even the most silly fancies. I have frequently warned him against such a course, but might just as well have spoken to the wind. My niece, is there anything in the city that you would like?"

" Oh yes, Aunt Fanny," exclaimed Hattie excitedly.

The eyes of the old maid brightened. "I'll get it for you, my dear, if it be anything that money can buy."

"It is not. Indeed, I thank you very much ; but do not ask any more questions, please. You could not gratify my wish, though ever so inclined."

Miss Wood looked both troubled and perplexed. "Are you sure that it cannot be procured ?" she inquired, "Almost everything can be bought in Toronto."

"You cannot buy that."

"Hattie, tell me what it is."

"So I would if you could get it for me ; but that is impossible."

"Then how foolish to take such whims into your head! I don't believe it is a *thing* at all, but some virtue; such as patience or persever-ance."

Mrs. Somerville smiled sadly. "Oh, no ; it is a substance," she said.

"Some great mansion, probably," returned Miss Wood in a peevish tone; "or a lovely park or garden."

" Oh, no, Aunt Fanny; it is a little thing that would lay on the palm of my hand."

" Jewellery! " exclaimed the spinster, in surprise, I thought you did not care for it."

" And very rightly."

"Suppose that little thing were in your hand now—"

" I would not part with it for all the jewellery in the world ! "

Miss Wood laughed. Hattie, your words include the Queen's crown, the old Regalia of Scotland, together with a vast amount of gold and precious stones. Now you might tell me what extraordinary thing it is you want."

" I would rather not, Aunt Fanny, for it is out of my reach and there is no good in wishing for it. However, do not feel curious about it ; for it is nothing extraordinary, but a simple little thing."

" A simple little thing ! " exclaimed the spinster, in a tone of disgust; " just as like as not, I would not value it sufficiently to give twenty-five cents for it."

" I am sure you would not."

o

" Hattie, I have no patience with you!" and the old maid arose and went off to her study.

A week passed over quietly.

" Aunt Fanny, you must put on your bonnet and cloak, please."

" Why, is this Division night ? "

" Yes, an open meeting for the installation of officers."

" Then I am willing to go. It will be a pleasure to see that ceremony again. Who is going to officiate ? Mr. Rose ? "

" Oh, no, Aunt Fanny," replied Mrs. Somerville, with a smile ; " he is Worthy Patriarch this term, and cannot very well install himself ! "

The spinster at once proceeded to get ready, and accompanied her niece to the Division-room.

The meeting was commenced by the members of Crystal Fountain singing the opening ode of the Sons of Temperance. Then, the Grand Worthy Patriarch, Mr. Caswell, with the assistance of Mr. Daniel Rose, proceeded to install the officers. Miss Wood looked on with great attention, while the subordinate stations were filled, one by one. It came last to the office of Worthy

Patriarch, and Mr. G. M. Rose stood up, placed his hand on his heart, and calmly took the oath.

Miss Wood whispered to her niece, " Does he not look perfectly self-possessed ? One would think he had been through that ceremony a dozen times before ! "

" Most probably he has," replied Hattie with a smile.

The new Worthy Patriarch, Mr. G. M. Rose, then proceeded to deliver his inaugural address. He thanked the members for the honour which they had conferred upon him in electing him to the office of Worthy Patriarch. He was not a novice, for it was twenty-seven years since he joined the Sons of Temperance, and a year afterwards he was elected Worthy Patriarch of his Division. Mr. Rose remembered well the night when he joined the Order; how nervous he was when he got up to make his first speech—it was only to second a motion, but he trembled like an aspen leaf, and was glad to take his seat again. Twenty-five years was a long while; it was the one-third of a man's life. Very many did not live to the age of seventy-five. Mr. Rose said he had as much faith in the organization as when first he joined it; he felt as young in the Order of the Sons of Temperance as he did twenty years ago. The association was instituted by selfish men— reformed drunkards, who cared not for their wives, children, nor even their sweet-hearts. But the Order they established was the best thing that ever happened for their wives, children and sweethearts. Was not that strange? Those men had signed the pledge in the old Washingtonian movement which was just like the Rine and Murphy movements of our day. When the wave had passed, sixteen men met in an upper room in New York—many most important events had taken place in upper rooms, and Mr. Rose instanced the wondrous results which flowed from the meeting of Christians in that upper room, more than eighteen hundred years ago—and great results flowed from the meeting of those sixteen men in New York. With them it was a serious question, whether they should give up their hopes of Heaven, which they had gained by signing the pledge. They resolved to hold on to their Temperance plank; and the result of that meeting was the organization of the Sons of Temperance. That was about thirty-five years ago. Since then, about two million people had signed the pledge through their instrumentality. Two million—that was one-half the population of our Dominion; and we must take into account the influence which those members exerted on all around them, before we could form a calculation of the amount of good accomplished by the Order. If any organization was raised up by Providence to do a great work, it was the Sons of Temperance. One of their objects was to save the drunkard. Reformed men, on signing the pledge, needed a place in which to spend their evenings instead of the bar-room, and this want was fully supplied by the Order. In Toronto, there was a meeting of some Division on every day in the week; and if a reformed man spent his nights among the Sons of Temperance, he did not see how he could possibly break his pledge, if at all in earnest. Another object was the teaching of the young. "Train up a child in the way he should go, and when he is old he will not depart from it." That was said by the wise

Solomon; and no truer words would ever go
down the ages. Mr. Rose then spoke of the legal
aspect of the subject, and earnestly remarked, "It
was not always so, *but now the chief aim and
object of the Sons of Temperance is Prohibition.*"

"Then you need never ask me to join, Hattie,"
peevishly observed Miss Wood.

Mr. Rose invited the outsiders who were present to give in their names and unite with the
Order. The ladies were only allowed to come in
as visitors some years ago; but when it was
found that they could actually behave themselves
in a Division-room, they were admitted to equal
rights with the men. ("We can behave ourselves
far better than they can;" muttered the spinster
with a scowl.) Mr. Rose spoke of the pleasant
evenings which were spent here; there was no
wrangling among the members, though, as a matter of necessity, there were sometimes differences
of opinion. It would never do for every one to
think alike. He then playfully remarked that
many youthful faces were turned anxiously towards him, as much as to say how well they would

like an opportunity for a talk with their next-door neighbour. He said they should soon have a chance. Then after again thanking the members for electing him to the office and promising that he would try to make the evenings as pleasant in the future as they had been in the past, Mr. Rose gravely announced an intermission of seven and a half minutes.

The young folks laughed, and immediately began to make the best use of their time. The Worthy Patriarch left his seat on the platform and went down among the audience. When the short recess had expired, he returned to his place and observed in a playful tone that he was glad to be able to inform them that the question had been popped in three cases, and another party said to him, " Mr. Rose, you did not give us time enough. Seven and a half minutes was too short ; so we have taken until to-morrow night to think over it." He advised the young people to bring their sweethearts with them and thus increase the strength of the Division.

Music and singing followed. Then Mr. Dil-worth read two of Will Carleton's Farm Ballads,

"Betsy and I are out;" and the sequel to the same.

Mr. Rose said there was something radically wrong in that family arrangement. If the husband had made it a rule to kiss his wife every morning before leaving home, it would not have been twenty years before the wife would have kissed him in return. The speaker was sure that Mr. Dilworth would not act in such a manner; indeed Mrs. Dilworth would not allow it. Mr. Rose proceeded to charge the various husbands among his audience to kiss their wives, and never to "let the sun go down upon their wrath," but always to go to bed in good temper.

Miss Wood whispered in a sarcastic tone to her niece, "I don't doubt that Mr. Rose is a model husband and father."

"Neither do I," gravely replied Hattie.

The spinster felt annoyed that Mrs. Somerville obstinately persisted in taking her ironical remarks in earnest, and rewarded her niece with a vigorous pinch.

On the way home, she snappishly inquired, "Won't Mr. Rose make a good Worthy Patriarch."

"Most excellent, Aunt Fanny."

" My niece, you are enough to make a saint lose his temper," crossly answered Miss Wood. " I never thought," she went on, " that those Sons of Temperance were so strongly in favour of Prohibition. I do not care for any total abstinence societies except the moral suasion clubs."

" Two years ago," said the Professor, " Mr. Rose joined one in Detroit, and donned their ribbon ; but finding they were anti-Prohibitionists, he immediately took it off."

" Consistent," muttered Miss Wood. " No sailing under false colours for him. Hattie," she added suddenly, turning to her niece, " don't you hate those enormous fur caps, like that which Ronald has on now. Do just give it a gentle pull and it will doubtless envelope his whole head and face."

Mr. McFarlane laughed. " It is not becoming to me I know," he said ; " but very comfortable for all that. Besides, there are few persons who look well in their winter garments."

" Oh, Ronald, don't you think that little dark fur cap which Mr. Rose wears, becomes him ? "

" Certainly I do, Hattie. There are some who look well in them, of course."

"I like it. His hair shows more plainly than in any hat he could wear."

"Yes," responded the spinster scornfully, "that 'beautiful' dark golden-red hair, which you described to your father. Of course you would like a lock of it!"

"I would, indeed, Aunt Fanny."

"And nothing would ever induce you to part with it!" added Miss Wood in bitter irony.

"Nothing would ever induce me to part with it!" emphatically returned Hattie.

The old maid was in a rage. "You don't mean a word you say—it is only to provoke me, I am sure of it. You remember enough of the Bible, my niece, to know that all liars shall have their part—"

Here Ronald thought best to interrupt the spinster, so he calmly observed, "I think, ma'am, you may safely give Hattie credit for speaking the truth. I am only sorry that it is impossible for me to grant her wish. Should it ever be in my power—"

"Now, don't you be foolish enough to make any such promise. The idle whims of my silly niece are innumerable. She will be teasing you for some of Neal Dow's hair next !"

The mere mention of the " father of the Maine Law" set Mrs. Somerville's thoughts off in another direction, and she earnestly inquired, " Aunt Fanny, don't you admire that picture of him, in the Division-room ? I have often wished for one just like it—"

" That old, yellow faded print ! What a horrible taste you have, Hattie; really, it gets worse instead of better. I suppose that the 'Maine Law' in all its beauty, printed on each side of him, gives a charm to the picture in your eyes."

" It does indeed. Do you remember the words of the Rev. Theodore Cuyler, 'The Prohibitory Law movement was, not long ago, in a minority of one ; but the Lord of Hosts stood with that man, and together they were more than an overmatch for all that were against them.' Aunt Fanny, '*that man*' was the Honourable Neal Dow !"

CHAPTER XX.

THE DOMINION ALLIANCE.

"YOU asked for those stones, Aunt Fanny, so here they are."

Miss Wood took the box from her niece and carefully surveyed the contents.

"So you were collecting specimens of rock instead of teaching Temperance to those young ones in North Hastings," said the spinster with a laugh. "Hattie, did anybody find out that you were a total abstainer?"

Mrs. Somerville looked surprised. "Why yes; do you suppose I was ashamed of my principles? Not in the least. I told them that I was a Good Templar before the first week was out."

"And, Good Templary was at a discount out there."

"It was—most decidedly."

"So you were contented with being a total abstainer yourself, and out of school-hours devoted your time to study."

"Yes, Aunt Fanny, but such a course seems very selfish to me now."

The old maid looked sharply at her niece, as she remarked, abruptly, "Hattie, I should not like that Central Club to go down. It is wrong to blame the whole society for the evil conduct of a few. Now, answer me some questions. How many were present at the election of officers last summer? It was a poor meeting, being held just after the Club had split in two—"

"There were one hundred members or more."

"Very good. Now, how many put in an appearance at that last so-called election?"

"Counting the late comers, there were thirty persons, I believe."

"A miserable little meeting truly; a cut-and-dried scheme, spite work, I have no doubt. A more fitting opportunity could scarcely have presented itself, for two or three factious persons to lead a number of ignorant men by the nose. That all was done fairly and squarely, I will never believe."

"You must remember, Aunt Fanny, that even in that 'miserable little meeting,' as you justly call it, there were men such as Mr. Walker, who voted for Mr. Rose, and would on no account have cast a ballot against him."

"I am glad to hear it. Though I dislike Prohibition, my niece, you must know me well enough to feel assured that I hate ingratitude. You will still take some little interest in the Club, though, of course, you cannot have much confidence in several of those who have now the controlling power."

"Oh, we will attend some of the meetings, Aunt Fanny, but—"

"But what?"

"It is utterly impossible for me to feel the same towards that Club as I did before. Once in three weeks or so, if all be well, Ronald and I will go to the Executive meeting, to watch the present delectable set of officers, especially that new Treasurer."

"Do you include the President?"

"Oh, no; Mr. Hassard needs no watching. Now, do hurry, Aunt Fanny; I want you this afternoon."

"Indeed?"

"To attend the Convention of Temperance men, which was called by the Dominion Alliance."

"A likely thing. A meeting of Prohibitionists."

"You must come. Mr. Rose will take part in the discussions, at least it is to be hoped so."

The spinster frowned. "You must excuse me, Hattie, I cannot go."

Mrs. Somerville knew that it was useless to press the matter. After a few moments of earnest thought, she inquired, "Aunt Fanny, why is it that our Dominion Alliance and the National Temperance Society of the United States are not on a good financial basis, like the United Kingdom Alliance of Great Britain?"

"Oh, because England is an old and wealthy country, far more so than either Canada or the States."

"That may be one reason, but there are others as well. Both ministers and members of churches give our cause the cold shoulder, as a general

thing. They can, however, raise funds to build
costly edifices in which to worship God, no matter at what expense of time or trouble. Aunt
Fanny, you know that bazaar of Mr. Handford's
Church, which was held a short time ago ?"

"Yes; you were devoutly wishing that the
proceeds were for Temperance purposes, more
especially to advance Prohibition. I coaxed you
to accompany me to Shaftesbury Hall, but in vain.
My niece," added the spinster, in a tone of con-
tempt, "the ladies of Canada care nothing about
Prohibition."

"Oh, they do, Aunt Fanny !"

"Actions speak louder than words, my dear.
If so, why do they not assist in raising funds to
put that Dominion Alliance in a position for
practical work ? Answer me that."

Mrs. Somerville was puzzled and made no reply. On her return from the first session of the
Convention, she informed her Aunt that "the
time was entirely taken up with a long discussion
about the Scott Act; and the desirability of sub-
mitting it as soon as practicable."

"Are you going to the mass meeting ?"

" I cannot very well, Aunt Fanny, on account of Crystal Fountain Division. I do wish that you would attend, and tell me all about it, for Edward Carswell is going to speak."

" I shall not do anything of the kind."

When Hattie returned, she said, "Our Worthy Patriarch, Brother Rose, was unavoidably absent, attending a church meeting of importance. An old member of Crystal Fountain was present, who now resides in Weston. He spoke in glowing terms of Brother G. M. Rose, and of the amount of 'Temperance work he was doing, in a quiet way, without saying a word about it.' Mr. Dilworth cordially endorsed the remarks of the member, and added that ' Mr. Rose gave more time and money to the Temperance Cause than any other man in Canada.' "

The spinster smiled. " I suppose that such an eulogium partly made amends to you for the disappointment of not hearing Edward Carswell at the mass-meeting."

" Yes, Aunt Fanny, I was glad, of course."

On the following night, Miss Wood remarked, " Now, just give me a brief outline of those three

P

sessions to-day which you have so *faithfully* attended."

" There was first a lengthy discussion relative to sending out agents of the Alliance; then, various other items of business came up, and the Provincial Branch for Ontario was formed. Mr. Rose would not take the office of Treasurer. He is one of the Executive Committee, however; and as for Secretaries, they have got two admirable ones, viz., Mr. Thomas Webster, Grand Scribe of the Sons of Temperance, and Mr. Casey, of the *Casket*, Grand Worthy . Secretary of the Good Templars. Some persons were silly enough to object, because 'outsiders,' who belonged to neither Order, might take offence. Mr. Rose was willing to have any number of nominations, but wanted the best men in such important places. He hotly denounced the fault-finding class of outsiders as 'croakers.' The chairman (Rev. Mr. Dewart) called him to order, because that was not 'parliamentary language.' 'Then it's *clerical*!' retorted Mr. Rose, immediately resuming the debate."

Miss Wood laughed. "Well," she said. "I

own it was provoking. Some men have no sense at all and would put incapable men in important positions, where they would effectually spoil every good plan that could be devised."

"This evening," continued Hattie, "a member spoke of the proposed repeal of the Dunkin By-law in York County."

. "What does Mr. Rose think now?" eagerly inquired Miss Wood.

"He evidently thinks it better than any license law, Aunt Fanny, and would like counties to hold on to it, until they get the Scott Act. The licensed victuallers are pressing the repeal in York—"

" Well, go on."

"Mr. Rose's emphatic advice to the members was, ' *Oppose the repeal, fight them to the last!*' "

"Just what one might have expected from him," muttered the spinster.

"Aunt Fanny, I am sorry that you were not there, for the meetings were really enjoyable. Many of the men were life-long workers in the cause; and some of them so old that they need never expect to see Prohibition carried. But such

may say, with that aged veteran, the Hon. Edward Delavan, who has gone home to his rest, 'I
shall not live to see it, but I trust to hear the
triumph on earth re-echoed by the angels in Heaven!' "

THE END.

www.ingramcontent.com/pod-product-compliance
Lightning Source LLC
Chambersburg PA
CBHW020117030726
47498CB00006B/2147